Usborne
Illustrated
Grimm's
Fairytales

Usborne
Illustrated
Grimm's
Fairytales

Ruth Brocklehurst
and Gillian Doherty

Illustrated by Raffaella Ligi

Designed by Mary Cartwright
and Jessica Johnson

Contents

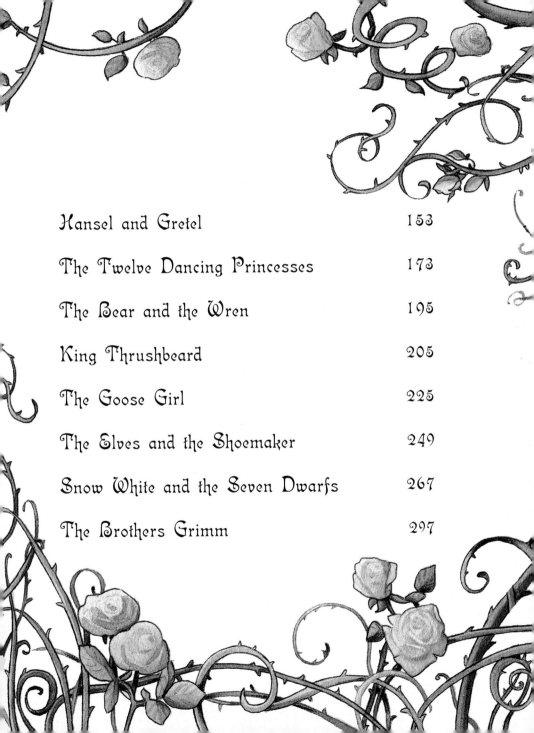

Snow White and Rose Red

Snowflakes swirled down from the night sky. It was bitterly cold. But inside the little cottage at the edge of the forest a welcoming fire glowed.

Snow White and her sister Rose Red were huddled beside the fire, listening carefully. Their mother was telling them a story. Suddenly, there was a knock at the door. "Who can be out on a night like this?" said Snow White.

"I'll go and see," said Rose Red. She opened the door and let out a scream. Towering over her was an enormous black bear.

"Don't be afraid," said the bear softly. "I won't hurt you. I just want to warm myself a little beside the fire."

"Poor bear," said the mother. "Forgive my daughter. Come inside and make yourself at home."

"Thank you," replied the bear. He dropped down onto all fours and shook his shaggy coat, sending snowflakes showering everywhere.

Snow White watched nervously as the huge beast lumbered over and settled down on the rug. She had never seen a bear before.

At first, the two sisters kept their distance, but the bear seemed so gentle that their fear soon fell away. Slowly, they crept closer to get a better look at him.

The bear lifted his sleepy head. "Why don't you sit beside me?" he murmured.

Feeling bolder, they kneeled down and stroked his thick fur. The bear gave a contented growl.

Gradually, the growling became a snore. Snow White and Rose Red snuggled up to him and, before long, all three of them were fast asleep.

When morning came, the bear padded into the forest, leaving a trail of giant pawprints behind him in the snow.

"You will come back, won't you?" begged Snow White as they waved goodbye.

"If you'll have me," the bear called back over his shoulder.

The next night he returned, and the night after, and for many nights after that.

Snow White and Rose Red looked forward to his visits more and more. They fed him honey buns, tickled his tummy and played hide and seek. In return, the bear gave them rides on his back and showed them how to make a den.

But time passed by quickly. The snow melted away and a carpet of bluebells spread across the forest. Spring had arrived.

"I'm afraid I must go away for a while," announced the bear one morning.

"Why?" cried Snow White. "Have we done something to upset you?"

"Of course not," replied the bear. "I have to go and guard my treasure from the wicked dwarfs in the forest. During the winter, when the ground is frozen, they hide away in their caves. But, now that spring is here, they'll come out and make mischief."

Snow White and Rose Red tried to change their friend's mind, but nothing they could say would persuade him to stay. Burying their faces in his fur, they hugged him tightly. "We'll miss you," they said.

"I'll miss you too," said the bear tenderly. "But I'll be back as soon as I can."

They opened the door and the bear slipped outside. As he did, his fur caught on the bolt and a piece tore off.

Snow White saw a flash of gold beneath, but before she could say anything, the bear had disappeared into the forest.

A few days later, Snow White and Rose Red went into the forest to collect some firewood. They hadn't gone far when they caught sight of a strange little creature hopping up and down in the long grass.

As they got closer, they realized that it was a dwarf. He had a long, white beard and an angry, pink face. "Is there something wrong?" asked Rose Red.

"Of course there's something wrong," he snapped. "Can't you see my beard is trapped?"

Rose Red looked and saw that the dwarf's beard was tangled up in some brambles. "Oh dear," she said. "How did that happen?"

"I haven't got all day to stand around answering your foolish questions," he grumbled. "Hurry up and set me free."

Snow White and Rose Red gave the dwarf's beard a tug, but it was no use.

"Wait," said Snow White. "I've got an idea." She reached into her pocket and pulled out her sewing scissors. Then, with a snippety-snip, she chopped off the end of his beard.

"You silly goose!" he howled. "Look what you've done to my lovely beard."

Snow White opened her mouth to reply, but the dwarf was already busy scrambling under the bush. He pulled out a bag of gold and slung it over his shoulder. Muttering and spluttering, he stomped away.

A few days later, Snow White and Rose Red went down to the river to catch some fish for supper. "Look over there," said Rose Red. "It's that funny little man again."

Sure enough, there was the dwarf, jumping up and down among the reeds like a crazy frog. This time, he'd managed to get his beard caught up in his fishing line.

"Not you two again," he groaned when he saw them. "You bring nothing but bad luck."

Just then, a hungry fish came along and swallowed the worm on the end of the fishing line. As it tried to swim away, the dwarf found himself being dragged towards the water's edge. "Don't just stand there, you lazy lumps. Do something!" he shrieked.

Snow White and Rose Red rushed over to help, but try as they might they couldn't free him. Once again, Snow White took out her scissors and, with a snippety-snip, she chopped off some more of his beard.

"What did you do that for?" the dwarf exploded. "There's nothing left of it. I'll never be able to show my face again." Without another word, he fished a bag of pearls from among the reeds and marched off.

A few weeks later, Snow White and Rose Red were on their way into town when they spotted an eagle flying low over the fields. It circled around and around. Then, suddenly, it swooped down behind a hedge.

The two girls heard a cry and ran to see what was happening.

"Let me go!" came an irritable voice. It was the dwarf again. The eagle had seized him in its claws and was about to fly away.

"Leave him alone!" shouted Rose Red boldly. But the eagle took no notice. Beating its mighty wings, it lifted the dwarf right off the ground.

Quickly, Rose Red grabbed the dwarf's coat while Snow White held on to Rose Red's waist. The eagle pulled one way and the two sisters pulled the other, dragging the dwarf to and fro.

After a few minutes of tug-of-war, the eagle finally let go, and the dwarf tumbled down to the ground.

Grumbling loudly, he scrambled to his feet and dusted himself down. "Look at the state of my coat," he complained. "Clumsy oafs! You should be more careful."

Then, picking up a bag of jewels from underneath the hedge, the dwarf stormed away.

Snow White looked at Rose Red and they both shrugged. "There's just no pleasing some people," said Rose Red.

When they were on their way home later that afternoon, Snow White and Rose Red came across the dwarf yet again. This time he was crouching down, counting something on the ground. He tried to hide it, but it was too late.

The two girls stopped and stared. Scattered in front of him were thousands of diamonds, rubies, emeralds and sapphires, all shimmering and sparkling in the sunlight.

"What do you think you're looking at?" yelled the dwarf. He picked up a rock and was about to throw it at them when he heard a low growl behind him.

The dwarf spun around and saw a huge black bear heading straight towards him. It was baring its teeth menacingly.

There was no time to run, so he had to think quickly. "Please spare me, Mr. Bear," he begged. "A little creature like me would hardly provide a mouthful for such a great beast. You should take these two girls instead. They'd make a much tastier dinner."

The bear gave an angry snort. It raised its paw and struck the dwarf with all its might. The dwarf staggered, and fell to the ground, stone dead.

Snow White and Rose Red turned to run away. "Wait! Don't be afraid," called the bear. "I won't hurt you."

The girls stopped in their tracks. His voice was familiar. Filled with excitement, they turned to greet their old friend.

But the bear was no longer there. In his place was a handsome young man dressed in fine robes. "Who are you?" gasped Snow White.

"I am a prince," he answered. "That evil dwarf bewitched me and then stole all my father's treasure. For more than a year, I have roamed the forest as a bear. Only his death could set me free. Now, at last, the spell is broken."

Snow White hung her head sadly.

"Is something wrong?" asked the prince. "I thought you'd be pleased for me."

"I am," said Snow White. "It's just that I'll miss our friend the bear."

"I'm just the same inside," said the prince, "and I hope I'll become your friend too."

Snow White smiled. "You already are," she answered shyly.

In fact, they became much more than friends. They fell in love, and a few years later they were married in his father's palace.

Since Snow White and Rose Red had always been inseparable, you won't be at all surprised to hear that she married the prince's brother, and of course they all lived happily ever after.

Little Red Riding Hood

It was washing day at the farmhouse. A warm breeze was blowing, and a red hood and cloak fluttered on the line.

A little girl skipped out of the house to bring in the washing. First, she unpegged the red hood. She pulled it over her dark curls and tied it under her chin. Then, she took down a matching red cape and put that on too.

The little girl loved her red hood and cape so much that she wore them all the time, except when her mother insisted that they absolutely had to be washed. And so everyone always called her Little Red Riding Hood.

The girl took down the rest of the washing and went back inside. The kitchen was filled with the warm smell of baking.

Little Red Riding Hood's mother was at the table, packing a basket with food. She put in a freshly baked cake, some fruit, some soft, creamy cheese and a jar of honey.

"Who's that for, Mother?" asked Little Red Riding Hood, cheerfully.

"It's for your grandmother," her mother replied. "She isn't feeling very well, so this food will do her good."

"Shall I take it to her?" Little Red Riding Hood suggested. "I can keep her company for a while to cheer her up."

"That's a lovely idea," agreed her mother. "What a thoughtful girl you are." She handed her daughter the food basket and straightened her red hood.

"Now be careful and hurry straight there," she said. "And don't forget what I've taught you: never stray from the path, and never, ever talk to strangers."

"I won't," promised Little Red Riding Hood.
She kissed her mother goodbye, and set off for
her grandmother's cottage in the forest.

Little Red Riding Hood swung the basket of
food and hummed a little tune as she skipped
along the path. It was a beautiful spring
morning. The sun was shining, birds were
singing and the air was sweet with the perfume
of flowers.

She had been to her grandmother's house
hundreds of times, but she'd never made
the journey on her own before. The deeper she
went into the forest, the taller the trees seemed
to grow, and the darker it became.

Little Red Riding Hood began to feel a little
nervous, imagining all kinds of scary creatures
lurking in the shadows. Her skip broke into

a jog, and then her jog broke into a run. She was
in such a hurry that she nearly ran straight into
a huntsman.

"Good morning, Little Red Riding Hood,"
he said. "What brings you to the forest today?"

Little Red Riding Hood smiled. She liked
the huntsman, and was relieved to see a familiar
face. "My grandmother isn't feeling very well,
so I'm taking her this basket of food," she told
him. "It's the first time I've walked there all
by myself," she added.

"What a kind, brave girl you are," said the huntsman. "I'm going that way myself so we can walk together if you like."

"That would be lovely," beamed Little Red Riding Hood. With the huntsman beside her, the forest didn't seem so dark and scary after all.

"So what are you doing in the forest today?" she asked the huntsman.

"I'm trying to catch a big, bad wolf," he replied. "He's a terrible nuisance, sneaking into people's farmyards, wrecking their vegetable patches and stealing their animals."

"Oh dear," gasped Little Red Riding Hood. "I hope you catch him soon."

Before long, they came to a fork in the path. "This is the turn to my grandmother's house," said Little Red Riding Hood. "Thank you for walking with me. I'll be fine on my own from here." So the huntsman said goodbye and went on his way.

Alone again, Little Red Riding Hood looked around. "It's such a beautiful day," she thought. "And my poor grandmother is stuck in bed. A pretty bunch of flowers will cheer her up."

Forgetting what her mother had told her, Little Red Riding Hood ran off the path to a cluster of nodding bluebells. She picked one, then she saw some sunny yellow daffodils a little further off.

Each time she picked a flower, she saw an even prettier one, further on. And so she went deeper and deeper into the forest away from the path.

The little girl was so busy picking flowers
that she nearly ran straight into a wolf. Yelping,
she jumped back in fright. She'd never seen
a wolf before.

"Good morning, little girl," said the wolf.
"What are you doing in this deep, dark forest all
by yourself?"

"I'm sorry," Little Red Riding Hood replied,
nervously. "I'm not supposed to talk to
strangers. Especially not to big, bad wolves."

"But I'm not a big, bad wolf," he lied
through his teeth. "I'm a nice, friendly wolf.
In fact, the huntsman is a friend of mine."

The wolf seemed so charming and polite,
Little Red Riding Hood didn't think there could
be any harm in talking to him. So she told him,
"My grandmother lives in a little cottage nearby.

She's not feeling very well, so I'm taking her this basket of food, and picking a bunch of flowers for her bedside."

"What a nice little girl you are," said the wolf. He licked his lips, thinking, "What a tasty meal she'd be. If I can get to the old woman's cottage first, I'll be able to eat the girl and her grandmother for lunch."

"Just look at those beautiful buttercups over there," said the wolf, "and those daisies a little further on. Wouldn't they look lovely in your bunch of flowers?"

"Oh, yes," agreed Little Red Riding Hood. And she ran over to pick some.

The wolf watched the little girl disappear into the forest. Then he raced ahead to her grandmother's cottage and knocked on the door.

"Who's there?" came a frail, old voice
from inside.

"It's your granddaughter," said the wolf in
a girlish voice. "I've brought you a basket of
food for lunch."

"What a sweet girl you are, Little Red Riding
Hood," the old woman called
back. "Please let yourself
in. I'm too weak to get
out of bed."

So the wolf pushed
open the door and
stepped into
the cottage.

Without saying another word, the wolf
went straight to the poor old woman's bed
and gobbled her up.

The wolf belched. "Now I just have to wait for the little girl," he thought, looking around the old woman's cottage for a place to hide.

He tried to crouch under the table, but it was too low. He tried to squeeze into the dresser, but it was too narrow. Then he had an idea.

The big, bad wolf wrapped the old woman's shawl around his shoulders, put on her spectacles, pulled her night cap down to his ears and climbed into her bed, drawing the quilt right up to his nose.

His mouth watered and his stomach rumbled as he lay waiting for his next course to arrive.

By the time Little Red Riding Hood had gathered as many flowers as she could carry, it was almost lunchtime. She quickly retraced her steps back to the path and hurried to her grandmother's cottage.

Little Red Riding Hood stopped outside the house. "That's strange," she thought. "Grandmother doesn't normally leave her door wide open." She knocked on the open door.

"Who's there?" called a muffled voice.

"It's Little Red Riding Hood," she answered, stepping inside and closing the door behind her. "I've brought you a basket of food and a bunch of flowers," she said.

"What a lovely girl you are," came the voice from under the bed covers.

"Oh dear," thought Little Red Riding Hood. "Grandmother must be really sick. She doesn't sound right at all." When she walked over to the bed, she got a terrible shock. Her grandmother didn't look right either.

"Oh, Grandmother, what big ears you have," said Little Red Riding Hood.

"All the better to hear you with," came the muffled reply.

"What big eyes you have," she added.

"All the better to see you with," said the wolf, sitting up and giving her a wide, toothy grin.

"What big teeth you have," Little Red Riding Hood gasped in alarm.

"All the better to eat you with!" cried the wolf. And, with that, he sprang out of bed and swallowed the little girl whole – hood, cloak and all.

The wolf patted his full, round belly and gave a satisfied belch. "Now I could do with a little nap," he yawned. So he climbed back into the bed and fell sound asleep.

A little while later, the huntsman came by. "I'll just see if the old woman needs anything," he thought. So he knocked softly on the door. But the only reply he got was a loud, growling snore. "I've never heard an old woman snore like that before," thought the huntsman. "I'd better make sure she's all right."

He peered through the window and there, snoring away on the bed, lay the big, bad wolf. "At last, I've caught him!" cried the huntsman and he crept into the cottage.

There was no sign of Little Red Riding Hood or her grandmother. "Could the wolf have eaten them?" he wondered. "If he did, I might be able to save them." He took a large pair of scissors from the dresser, and began to cut open the wolf's bulging belly.

Snip. A flash of red velvet appeared. Snippety snip. Out sprang Little Red Riding Hood. Snip snippety snip. Up popped her grandmother, looking very confused.

"Thank you for rescuing us," cried Little Red Riding Hood, hugging the huntsman. "It wasn't at all nice in there."

While the wolf was still asleep, they came up with a cunning plan. The huntsman collected a large pile of rocks. Little Red Riding Hood stuffed them into the wolf's belly. Then her grandmother sewed it all up.

"This ought to teach that troublesome wolf a lesson he won't forget," declared the huntsman.

Just then, the wolf woke up. "Ooh, something I ate has really disagreed with me," he groaned, rubbing his belly. "I must have indigestion."

As the wolf rolled out of bed, the rocks rattled noisily inside him.

"What's wrong with me?" asked the wolf.

"We've sewn rocks into your belly," giggled Little Red Riding Hood. "Now everyone will hear you coming. So you won't be able to creep around stealing people's animals ever again."

The wolf was furious. "You're even sneakier than I am," he complained, and he stomped off into the forest, muttering and spluttering, while the rocks clattered inside him.

With his belly full of rocks, the big, bad wolf had to change his ways. He made such a noise wherever he went that the local farmers paid him to work in their fields as a scarecrow.

And from that day on, Little Red Riding Hood never again forgot what her mother had taught her: not to stray from the path, and never, ever talk to strangers – especially not to big, bad wolves.

Rapunzel

All around the enchantress's house there were high, forbidding walls, but beyond them lay a beautiful garden. The miller and his wife could see into it from their bedroom window, although they had never dared to set foot inside.

Then, when the miller's wife found she was having a baby, she began to crave all kinds of unusual foods.

One morning, she looked out of her window and spotted a leafy, green plant growing in the enchantress's garden. "Look at that lovely rapunzel," she said to her husband. "I must have some to make into a salad."

"Erm...I'm not sure that's such a good idea," said her husband nervously. "How about some nice cheese instead?"

His wife shook her head. No other food could tempt her. As the days went by, she grew pale and miserable.

The miller loved his wife dearly and hated to see her so unhappy. Even though he was afraid, he decided to try to get some rapunzel for her.

He waited until it was dark, and then
clambered over into the enchantress's garden.
Luckily, she was nowhere to be seen.

Tiptoeing over to
where the rapunzel
grew, the miller picked
the juiciest leaves and
put them in his pouch.
Then he climbed back
over the wall.

His wife was absolutely
delighted when he brought
her the rapunzel. She chopped
up the leaves with some tomatoes
and lettuce, and ate it all for her
supper. But the salad was so tasty that it
only made her long for more.

The next evening, the miller climbed into the garden once again. Hurriedly, he picked the rapunzel and turned to go, but to his horror the enchantress was blocking his way.

Her stony eyes seemed to stare right into his soul. "How dare you steal my rapunzel!" she stormed. "You'll pay for this with your life."

"I'm t-t-terribly sorry," stammered the miller. "It's for my wife. She's going to have a baby."

The enchantress's face softened. "Well, why didn't you say so?" she said. "In that case, you may help yourself to as much rapunzel as you like. There's just one condition."

"What is it?" asked the miller fearfully.

"When the baby is born, you must give it to me," replied the enchantress.

The miller was so terrified that he didn't dare to refuse. He was just happy to escape alive.

Scrambling back over the wall, he hurried to his wife and gave her the rapunzel, but he didn't tell her what had happened.

The months went by, and the miller and his wife looked forward to the birth of their baby. He tried to forget about the promise he had made, but his happiness was overshadowed by his dark secret.

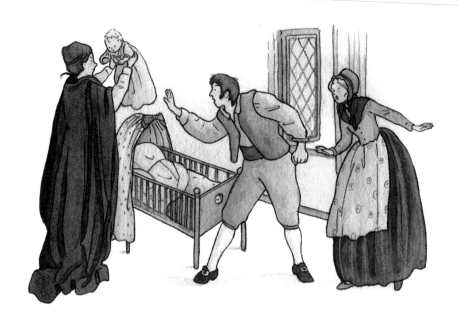

The very day the miller's wife gave birth,
the enchantress appeared in the nursery.
"Hand over the child," she demanded.

The baby started to cry. "Leave us alone,"
shouted the miller. "You've no business here."

"A deal is a deal," snarled the enchantress,
"and I've come to collect my payment." Pushing
him aside, she snatched the baby out of the crib
and vanished into thin air.

She named the baby Rapunzel, after the plant the miller had stolen from her. As the child grew up, the enchantress treated her like a slave and never let her out of her sight.

The years went by and Rapunzel became more and more beautiful. Her golden hair shone like the sun itself. It grew thick and fast, tumbling over her shoulders, past her waist and right down to her feet.

Yet still Rapunzel's hair kept on growing. Eventually, she had to tie it up just to stop it from getting tangled.

"That girl's getting far too pretty," thought the enchantress one morning, as she watched her scrubbing the floor. "If I'm not careful, some handsome young man will come along and fall in love with her."

So, she imprisoned Rapunzel in a tower
in the middle of the forest. Escape was out of
the question. The tower had no door or staircase,
and the only window was high up in the walls.

When the enchantress wanted to go in, she
stood at the bottom and called out, "Rapunzel,
Rapunzel, let down your hair."

At this, Rapunzel unfastened her hair and
let it fall down to the ground. The enchantress
grabbed hold of it and hauled herself up.

A whole year went by, and not a soul came
near, apart from the enchantress. There was
nothing to do up in the tower, so Rapunzel
would often sing to amuse herself.

One day, quite by chance, a young prince was
riding by when he heard her sweet voice drift
down on the breeze.

The prince stopped to listen. Rapunzel's song was so beautiful and sad that it touched his heart. He circled the tower looking for a door, but there wasn't one.

He was about to call up to the window when he heard someone coming. Quickly, he hid behind a tree.

The enchantress marched to the tower. "Rapunzel, Rapunzel, let down your hair," she commanded.

To the prince's surprise, a golden braid tumbled down from the window, and the enchantress used it to haul herself up.

The prince waited for her to leave. Then he decided to try the trick for himself. "Rapunzel, Rapunzel, let down your hair," he called up to the window.

Down tumbled Rapunzel's golden braid once again. The prince took hold of it and began to climb up.

When Rapunzel realized that it wasn't the enchantress, she let out a cry of fear.

"I'm sorry. I didn't mean to frighten you," said the prince as he reached the top. "I heard your singing and had to see you."

He climbed in through the window and soon the two of them were chatting away like old friends. "It's nice to have someone to talk to," said Rapunzel mournfully. "I get so lonely up here. How I wish I could escape."

"Perhaps I can help you," said the prince. So the two of them put their heads together and between them they came up with a plan.

Each evening, the prince came to the tower and brought with him a ball of silk. Secretly, Rapunzel began to weave a ladder from it.

The weeks went by, and the ladder grew longer and longer. It was almost time for Rapunzel to make her escape.

Then, one day, the enchantress arrived at her usual time. "Rapunzel, Rapunzel, let down your hair," she called. So Rapunzel did.

As the enchantress climbed up, she tugged so hard that she almost pulled Rapunzel's hair out by the roots.

"Ouch! You're so much rougher than the prince," grumbled Rapunzel.

"What was that?" shrieked the enchantress.
"Wicked girl! So you've had a visitor have you?
Well, I'll make sure it never happens again."
In an instant, she whipped out a pair of scissors
and cut off Rapunzel's hair.

"Oh!" cried Rapunzel in horror.
"My hair! It's all gone."

"I haven't finished
with you yet, young
lady," the enchantress
snapped. Waving her
wand, she muttered
some mysterious words
under her breath.

A moment later, Rapunzel found herself
stranded in a hot, parched desert. There was
endless nothingness as far as the eye could see.

Meanwhile, the enchantress took Rapunzel's hair and tied it to the leg of the bed. Then she settled down to wait for the prince.

It wasn't long before she heard him cry, "Rapunzel, Rapunzel, let down your hair."

Keeping herself hidden, the enchantress threw the hair out of the window.

The prince took hold of it and began to climb up the tower. He reached the top and was halfway through the window before he saw the enchantress glowering at him.

"What have you done with Rapunzel?" he demanded.

"Have you come to rescue your pretty little sweetheart?" she mocked. "Well, you're too late. She's gone far away from here. You'll never see her again."

"Of course, if you're looking for a wife..." she added, leering at him.

This was too much for the prince. He tried to climb back down, but in his hurry he lost his grip.

Down he fell, tumbling head over heels. He would certainly have been killed if a thorn bush had not broken his fall. But, although it saved his life, the thorns scratched his eyes and blinded him.

The prince struggled to his feet. "I'll find Rapunzel somehow," he cried defiantly.

For months, the prince tried to find Rapunzel. He asked everyone he met whether they had seen her, but no one had.

Then, one day, he stopped at a market town on the edge of the desert. Through all the bustle and hubbub, he heard a voice so familiar that it made his heart leap with joy. "Rapunzel?" he called.

At the sound of her name, a golden-haired girl turned around. It was Rapunzel.

She ran to the prince and threw her arms around him. "Your poor eyes," she whispered. Gently, she kissed each one. As she did, tears rolled down her cheeks and fell into them.

The prince blinked and, in a blur of tears, her beautiful face appeared before him. "I can see you!" he exclaimed.

Kneeling down in the sand, he kissed her hand. "Now that I've found you, will you marry me?" he asked.

"Of course," answered Rapunzel without a moment's hesitation.

Everyone in the whole kingdom was invited to their wedding, including the miller and his wife. They were delighted to be reunited with their daughter at last, and she with them.

It was the happiest of days. The bells rang, the birds sang and the sun shone brightly. Luckily, the enchantress stayed away, and although she sulked for a very long time, she never bothered Rapunzel and the prince again.

Sleeping Beauty

Trumpeters blasted a joyful fanfare
and messengers rode out from the
castle to proclaim the news: the queen
had given birth to a baby girl.

The happy parents barely had eyes for anything except their newborn daughter. "She's the most beautiful thing I've ever seen," cooed the king. "What shall we call her?"

The queen gazed at the bloom of the baby's cheeks. They were as pink as the briar roses that grew in the garden.

"Let's call her Briar Rose," she suggested.

"A pretty name, for a pretty girl," the king agreed. "Yes, it suits her perfectly."

The king decided they should throw a party to celebrate, so he set about sending out invitations immediately. Everyone who was anyone was invited.

"Briar Rose must have a dozen fairy godmothers," he declared. "You never know when a little magic might come in handy." So he sent out twelve extra special invitations.

On the day of the party, a plush red carpet was rolled out for the guests as they flocked to the castle. Musicians struck up a merry tune, while acrobats leaped and tumbled among the party goers, and conjurers amazed them with card tricks. Then, they were shown to the dining hall, where they were treated to a fabulous feast.

After the feast, the fairy godmothers gathered around Briar Rose's cradle to bless her with magic gifts.

"Briar Rose will always be loving and kind," said the first, with a wave of her wand.

"Her beauty will be beyond compare," promised the second.

"And her honesty will be unfailing," added the third.

One by one, the fairy godmothers gave their blessings. But the last was interrupted.

"How dare you throw a party without inviting me!" came a shrill voice, cutting like a knife through the merry mood of the party. It was a wicked sorceress. She was wearing a storm-dark cloak, and her face was white with fury.

"I have a gift for Briar Rose," cackled the sorceress, brandishing her wand. "Before she celebrates her sixteenth birthday, the princess will prick her finger on a spinning wheel, and fall down dead!"

As soon as she had delivered her chilling curse, she vanished in a puff of smoke.

"Nooo!" wailed the king.

The queen broke down in inconsolable tears, while the rest of the room looked on in horrified silence.

Then, the last fairy godmother spoke up. "I haven't blessed the princess yet," she said. "My magic isn't powerful enough to undo the curse, but I can soften its blow."

She sprinkled magic dust over the cradle and gave her blessing. "Briar Rose will not die when she pricks her finger," she promised. "Instead, she and everyone else in the castle will fall into a deep sleep. Only a kiss from her true love will break the spell."

Even so, the king didn't want to take any chances with his precious daughter. So, as soon as his guests had gone home, he sent out orders for every spinning wheel in the kingdom to be destroyed. "If she can't prick her finger," he reasoned, "she won't come to any harm."

As the years went by, the fairy godmothers' wishes came true. Briar Rose grew to be kind and lovely in every way. Life in the castle was happy and carefree, and the princess reached her sixteenth birthday without coming near a single spinning wheel.

Thinking they'd managed to avoid the wicked sorceress's curse, the king decided it was safe to throw another party.

The castle was a rush of activity, as everyone prepared for the celebrations. The servants scrubbed the floors and polished the chandeliers until they sparkled and shone. The king sat on his throne wrapping a huge pile of birthday presents, and the queen brought in great armfuls of fragrant roses from the garden to decorate the castle.

Up in her room, Briar Rose was the most excited of all. This would be her very first ball. As she put on her rose-pink ball gown, she wondered what surprises the evening might have in store.

The princess straightened her tiara, and headed downstairs to join her parents. But, on the landing, her eye was caught by a strange, pale light.

Bursting with curiosity, she followed the light along the corridor and up a narrow, winding

staircase she'd never noticed before. The higher
she climbed, the brighter the light became.
At the very top of the stairs, she reached
an arched doorway.

Through the arch was a tiny attic bedroom.
In the far corner, an old woman sat hunched
over a spinning wheel. Briar Rose stepped into
the room and greeted the old woman gaily.

Of course, the princess had never seen
a spinning wheel before, so she asked,
"What are you doing?"

"I'm spinning wool into thread,"
replied the old woman. "Would you
like to try?" she asked, offering
the girl her stool.

"Yes please," replied Briar
Rose curiously.

"Here," said the old
woman. "Let me help
you." With an evil
cackle, she forced
Briar Rose's hand
onto the sharp
spindle of the
spinning wheel.

"Ouch!" cried
Briar Rose, jumping to her feet. "I've pricked my
finger." Suddenly, she felt faint and dizzy, and
the room seemed to spin around her. She
stumbled back and fell, lifeless, onto the bed.

Of course, the old woman was really the
wicked sorceress in disguise. She waved her wand
triumphantly and vanished in a puff of smoke.

But the princess wasn't dead. She had fallen

into a deep, enchanted sleep, just as the last fairy godmother had promised.

Sleep fell upon the castle, like a soft blanket. The king and queen slumped in their thrones, the guards started snoring at their posts and the cook nodded off over a cake she was decorating.

The kitchen cat became drowsy and let go of the mouse it had just caught, the horses dozed off in the stables and the doves in the rafters stopped cooing and tucked their heads under their wings. One by one, sleep overcame them all.

Even the clocks stopped ticking, their hands frozen at exactly the same time.

But time didn't stand still outside. Gradually, a tangle of thorns took over the garden. Each year, they grew higher and thicker until the castle was completely hidden from the outside world.

Across the land, the tale was told of an enchanted castle, where a beautiful princess lay sleeping, awaiting a kiss from her true love.

Princes came from far and wide to see if they could break the spell. They tried to hack through the thorns to reach the castle. But the harder they tried, the more the twisted branches seemed to bind together.

Eventually the princes gave up trying. A hundred years passed, and no one could remember whether the tale of the sleeping beauty was even true or just another fairy tale.

Then, one day, a prince from
a distant kingdom came riding by. His
great-grandfather had told him about
the sleeping princess, and he was determined
to rescue her.

Boldly, he approached the thorns. To his
astonishment, they were transformed into
rosebuds that sprang into bloom, right
in front his eyes.

As the prince stepped forward to
pick a flower, the branches unwound
themselves and opened up for him,
like welcoming arms.

The prince walked forward and found himself in the castle yard. He peered in at the horses asleep in the stables, stepped over the cat, and tiptoed past the snoring guards. In the great hall he saw the king and queen, slumped in their thrones. Their crowns had slipped down over their faces.

The prince searched for the princess all over the castle. At last, he came to the stairway leading up to the attic room where Briar Rose lay sleeping. His heart raced as he climbed the stairs and entered the room.

He gasped when he set eyes on the princess. She was so beautiful he could scarcely breathe. He stooped to kiss her.

The very moment his lips touched her cheek, her eyes flickered open and gazed into his.

"What's happened?" asked Briar Rose. "Have I been asleep?"

"You and everyone else in the castle have been asleep for a hundred years," replied the prince. "I've come to rescue you." And he told her all about the wicked sorceress's curse.

Downstairs, the rest of the household was waking up and springing back into action. The servants continued scrubbing and polishing, the cook brushed chocolate cream from her face and got back to decorating the cake, while the king and queen sat up in their thrones and straightened their crowns.

Briar Rose and the prince went down to the great hall. The prince told the king and queen what had happened, then he got down on one knee.

"Your majesties," he said, "Please may I have your daughter's hand in marriage?"

The king and queen were overjoyed.

"You have broken the spell, and proved you are our daughter's true love!" cried the queen.

"What are we waiting for?" the king exclaimed. "This calls for a celebration."

So, he ordered a fanfare and sent out messengers to proclaim the news: the curse had been lifted. It was time for another party.

The Frog Prince

It was a hot summer's evening, and the princess had found a shady spot among the trees beside a deep, blue pool.

Although she was already late for dinner, the princess was in no hurry to go home to the stuffy castle, so she lingered by the pool. Idly, she threw her golden ball into the air. It glinted in the evening sunlight, dazzling her. And, as she reached to catch it, her ball slipped from her fingers.

The princess watched helplessly as it landed in the pool with a plop, and vanished into the deep water. "My beautiful golden ball!" she cried. "How am I ever going to get it back?"

Then, she heard a croaky voice. "I can help you," it said.

The princess wiped the tears from her eyes, but she couldn't see anyone. "Who's there?" she called. "Where are you?"

"I'm right beside you," came the voice again.

The princess looked all around her, but she still couldn't see anyone.

"I'm down here, on this lily pad," called the voice.

The princess peered down at the lily pad. "Eugh! An ugly, slimy frog," she gasped. "And it can talk."

"I may not be pretty," croaked the frog. "But I'm really very nice, when you get to know me."

The princess stared at the frog's bulging eyes and gaping mouth in disbelief and disgust.

"I can get your ball back for you, Princess," the frog continued. "But will you do something for me in return?"

"I'll do anything you want," she replied. "I'll give you my pearls, my jewels, even my crown."

"I don't want any of those things," said the frog. "All I want in the world is a friend. But when you're an ugly, slimy frog, no one wants to know you. If you promise to be my best friend, take me to your castle let me eat at your table and sleep on your pillow, then I'll get your ball back for you."

"How ridiculous," thought the princess. "Who ever heard of a princess with a frog for a friend?" But to the frog she said, "I promise."

So the frog dived into the water. There was a huge splash, and rings of ripples spread out across the pool. The princess waited and watched as the ripples became smaller and smaller, until the water was as smooth as glass. She was about to give up and go home, when the frog burst out of the pool with her ball.

"Ta-da!" he croaked triumphantly, laying it at her feet.

"Thank you," cried the princess. She was so excited to have her precious ball back that she picked it up and ran straight home, without giving the frog a second glance.

The frog hopped after her as fast as he could. "Wait for me, I can't keep up," he called. "Take me with you to the castle, as you promised." But the princess had already left him far behind.

Back at the castle, the princess forgot all about the frog and sat down to dinner with the king and queen. They were about to start their soup, when they heard a knock at the door and a croaky voice calling, "Princess, it's your friend here for dinner. Please let me in."

The princess went to open the door. But when she saw the frog sitting on the doorstep, she squealed in disgust, and slammed the door in his face.

"Who was there?" asked the queen.

"Oh, it was no one," lied the princess, shifting nervously in her seat.

The king looked at her sternly over his spectacles. "Now, remember what I've taught you," he scolded. "Princesses always tell the truth."

"I'm sorry, Father," sighed the princess. "But it's only a horrible, slimy frog that wants to come in. And the dinner table's no place for pond life."

"Why's he here then?" asked the queen.

"Well…" began the princess, "I dropped my golden ball in a pond earlier. The frog said he'd get it back for me if I promised to be his friend and bring him back here for dinner."

"And did you promise?" asked the king.

"Yes, Father," she answered.

"How many times do I need to tell you? Princesses always keep their promises. And that includes you, young lady."

"Sorry, Father," muttered the princess, hanging her head in shame.

"And princesses are always polite to their

guests," the queen joined in. "Don't leave
the poor frog waiting outside. Let him in."

And so, the princess reluctantly opened
the door and went back to her seat. The frog
hopped in behind her and waited at the foot of
the table. Then he called, "Princess, please let me
up so I can eat with as you promised."

The princess hesitated. The thought of having
an ugly frog at the table was making her feel
slightly queasy. But the king gave her another of
his stern looks. So she pulled up a chair and piled
it high with cushions. Then she scooped up
the frog and dropped him onto the chair with
a shudder.

The frog made polite conversation and tried
not to make a mess as he lapped up his soup with
his long tongue. He slurped his stew and gulped

down his dessert as daintily as he could. "Please excuse my table manners," he said. "But frogs can't use knives, forks and spoons."

The king and queen said they didn't mind at all, but the princess was so disgusted that she barely touched her food.

After the dishes had been cleared away, the frog hopped down from the table. "That was delicious, thank you. But now I'm very tired," he yawned. "Princess, please will you take me to your room, so I can sleep on your pillow as you promised."

Again, the princess hesitated. She didn't want a cold, slimy frog anywhere near her pillow. But a princess always keeps her promises, and she didn't want another of her father's looks. So she picked up the frog and wearily climbed the stairs.

But, when they got to her room, the princess couldn't bear to let the frog on her nice, clean bed. So she put him down in the darkest corner of the room instead. "You can sleep here, Frog," she said. "Now I'm off to bed."

The frog watched forlornly as the princess climbed into her soft bed and pulled the downy quilt over her head. "Princess, I thought you were going to let me sleep on your pillow, and be my best friend," he said, and his voice cracked with disappointment.

Lying in her bed, the princess began to feel ashamed of the way she had treated the frog, and for breaking her promise to him. "He may be ugly and slimy," she thought to herself, "but he was kind to me, and I haven't been very friendly in return."

So, the princess got out of her bed and padded over to the frog. "I'm sorry I've been mean to you, Frog," she said, kneeling down beside him. She looked at the sorrowful creature and wondered, "Maybe a princess and a frog can be friends after all."

Gently, she scooped up the frog, carried him over to the bed, and placed him on her softest, plumpest pillow.

"You can sleep here, Frog," said the princess, soothingly. "And I will be your best friend – I promise."

But the instant the princess had spoken, there was a deafening boom, a blinding flash and a puff of smoke. The frog turned into a prince. He was tall and handsome, with sparkling green eyes and a kindly face.

The princess jumped back in fright, rubbing the stars from her eyes.

"Please don't be alarmed," said the prince. "I don't mean you any harm."

"First you're a frog that can talk, now you're a prince. What are you going to turn into next?" exclaimed the princess. "This is the strangest day I've ever known. Or is it all a dream?"

"No, it isn't a dream," replied the prince. "I really am a prince."

"And a very handsome one at that," sighed the princess, gazing into his eyes.

Just then, the king and queen burst into the room, almost tripping over one another in their haste.

"What's all the commotion?" asked the king, straightening his spectacles.

"We heard a terrible noise. Is something the matter?" the queen asked anxiously.

Then, they noticed the prince. "Who are you?" they asked in one voice.

"And what are you doing in my daughter's bedroom?" demanded the king. He gave the prince one of his sternest looks. "Explain yourself, young man."

And so, the prince told them all his story. "I come from the kingdom on the other side of the forest. One day, I was out walking when I came upon a glade where a wicked witch was busy casting spells. She was so angry with me for disturbing her that she cast a spell on me and turned me into a frog."

The princess gasped. "What happened next?" she asked.

The prince went on. "The witch told me that the only thing that could break her spell would be the love of a beautiful princess. But, she said no princess would ever make friends with an ugly, slimy frog, so I'd be stuck like that forever."

"But the wicked witch was wrong!" cried the king and queen proudly.

The prince, turned to the princess and got down on one knee. "Now you've saved me," he said, "I'd be very happy if you would marry me, and come to live in my castle, and be my best friend."

The princess beamed at the prince. "I'd like nothing better!" she exclaimed. "Besides, I've already promised to be your best friend, and everyone knows that princesses always keep their promises."

The Frog Prince

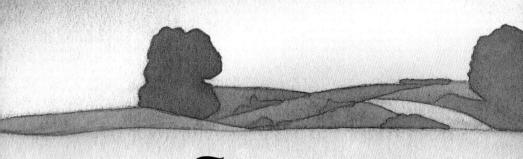

The Musicians of Bremen

The sun had just sunk below the horizon when the rooster began to crow from the top of his coop. His mournful cries sent the whole farmyard into confusion.

"Is it morning already?" asked the cat, lifting her sleepy head.

"It's not even night yet," said the dog.

"Why are you crowing at this time of day?" asked the donkey, looking out of the shed.

"I'm crowing for the last time," explained the rooster sadly. "Earlier, I overheard the farmer telling his wife to throw me in the cooking pot tomorrow."

The animals were shocked. "Who do these people think they are? They treat us like animals," they exclaimed.

"The farmer is always kicking me, and calling me lazy," said the dog.

"And he beats me if I don't pull his cart fast enough," added the donkey.

"His wife's mean, too" said the cat. "She wants to get rid of me because I'd rather curl up by the fire than go out catching mice."

The four creatures stared angrily at the farmhouse, where the farmer and his wife were just sitting down to their evening meal.

"We don't have to put up with this any more," declared the donkey. "Let's run away to Bremen to join the town musicians."

"What a good idea," said the rooster. "You can sing bass, the dog can sing tenor, and the cat and I can sing soprano."

The others agreed. So they watched and waited until the lights in the farmhouse were turned out. Then, in the dead of night, they stole out of the farmyard, crept down the lane and into the moonlit forest.

The animals walked deeper and deeper into the forest, until they came to a small clearing.

"Perhaps we should rest here," suggested the donkey. So he and the dog lay down under a tree, while the cat curled up in the crook of a low branch and the rooster found a perch right at the top.

"Can you see Bremen from up there?" asked the dog, hopefully.

The rooster scanned the horizon. "No," he called down, "but I can see a light up ahead, and it's coming from a cottage."

"Let's see if the people there might offer us some shelter for the night," said the donkey.

"It is rather cold out here," said the cat. "Perhaps they'll let us sit by their fire."

"And maybe they'll give us a little something to eat," added the dog, his stomach growling.

So they made their way to the cottage. The donkey, being the tallest and the bravest of the animals, peered in at the window to see what was going on inside.

"What can you see?" asked the rooster.

"There's a big table spread with all kinds of delicious food and drink," he replied. "And there are some mean-looking men sitting around it counting big sacks of money."

"If only it was us in there instead of them," sighed the dog.

"It can be," said the donkey. "I've got
an idea." He gathered the animals into a huddle
and told them his plan.

Then he stood at the window on his hind
legs, with his front hoofs propped up on
the ledge. Following his instructions, the dog
climbed up on the donkey's shoulders, the cat
jumped onto the dog's back and the rooster flew
up to perch on top of the cat's head.

They all held their breath, trying to keep
their balance until the donkey gave the signal,
"Now, sing!"

The donkey brayed, the dog howled,
the cat yowled and the rooster crowed, all at
the top of their lungs. The noise was so loud
that it shattered the glass, and the animals
burst through the window.

The men, who were
robbers, leaped from their seats. "Aargh!
We're being attacked by a four-headed
monster," one of them screamed.

"Run for your lives!" yelled another. They
shot out of the house and dived for cover in
the undergrowth among the trees.

The animals made themselves comfortable
in the cottage and started eating the robbers'
feast. When they had eaten and drunk their
fill, they each found a place to sleep.

The cat settled for a rug in front of
the fire and the dog lay down on the mat
by the door. The donkey found a soft pile
of straw out in the yard, while the
rooster flew up onto the roof.

Before long, they were all sound asleep.

Hiding out in the forest, the robbers began to feel cold and uncomfortable. The chief robber said, "Perhaps we shouldn't have been so hasty. I'm going to go back and see what's happening in there."

He crept to the cottage and tiptoed inside. It was so dark, he stubbed his toe on the table leg and woke the cat. Amid the gloom, he saw the cat's eyes shining by the fireplace and thought they were the last glowing embers of the fire. So he crouched down to light a match from them.

The cat didn't take kindly to being poked in the eye. She flew at his face, spitting and scratching. The robber jumped back in terror and tripped over the dog, who sank his teeth into the man's leg.

As the robber stumbled blindly out into the yard, and the donkey booted him in the backside with his hind legs. The man yelped in pain, and the donkey brayed back at him.

All the commotion woke up the rooster, who flew down from the roof in a flurry of feathers crowing a blood-curdling, "Cock-a-doodle-doo! Cock-a-doodle-doo!"

Scared out of his wits, the robber ran straight back to his gang. "What happened?" they asked.

"First, a witch spat at me and scratched me with her talons," he told them. "Then, I was stabbed by a knife-wielding fiend. After that, a big, black beast beat me with a club, and a blood-thirsty vampire flew after me, screeching, 'I'll get you! I'll get you!' I only just managed to fight them off."

The robbers never dared to go near
the cottage again. In fact, they left the forest
that very night and never returned. They left
behind so much food and money that the animals
lived the rest of their lives in luxury. They ate,
slept and sang whenever they wanted, but they
never did make it to Bremen.

Rumpelstiltskin

High on a hill, the windmill's sails turned steadily in the breeze. The proud old miller looked down on the village below.

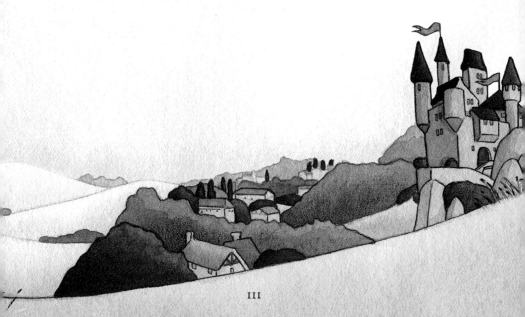

"It's about time my daughter was married,"
he thought. "But none of the young men in
the village can possibly match her."

The next day, the baker's son came to
the miller to buy a sack of flour. Spying the miller's
beautiful daughter working at her spinning wheel,
he asked her father shyly whether
he might ask her to marry him.

"My girl is far too good for a baker boy,"
scoffed the miller. "She's the prettiest girl in
the village and she spins the finest thread in
the entire kingdom. In fact," he boasted,
getting carried away, "she can even spin straw
into gold!"

Disappointed, the baker's son heaved his sack
of flour over his shoulder and trudged home.

Back in the village, the baker's son told his

mother what the miller had said. "That's incredible!" she said. She hurried off to tell the shoemaker's wife, who told the innkeeper, who told the king's huntsman.

It wasn't long before word of the girl's extraordinary skill reached the king. "A girl who can spin straw into gold!" he exclaimed. "This I have to see."

And so, the miller's daughter was summoned to the castle. "I hear you can spin straw into gold," said the king. "So I'm going to put you to the test. If you fail, your father will be punished."

He snapped his fingers and a guard whisked the girl away to a small room. It was piled high with straw, and in the middle there was low wooden stool and spinning wheel.

"Now get to work," ordered the guard. "You have until morning to spin this straw into gold." Then he left, locking the door behind him to make sure the girl didn't cheat.

The miller's daughter sat on the stool and sighed. She didn't want her father to be punished, but she didn't have a clue how to spin straw into gold. "Oh, what shall I do?" she cried.

All of a sudden, a peculiar little man appeared. He had pointed ears and his spindly legs looked as though they would snap under the weight of his round tummy. "What are you wailing about?" he demanded sharply.

Rumpelstiltskin

"I have to spin all this straw into gold," she replied. "But I don't know how."

"Pah! Is that all? I can help you," he said, narrowing his eyes. "But what will you give me in return?"

"Here," she said, taking off her necklace. "You can have my locket."

"That'll do nicely!" said the little man, snatching the necklace from her.

Grabbing a handful of straw, he set to work. Whirr, whirr, whirr went the wheel, as it began to spin.

The miller's daughter watched in amazement as the straw turned into bright gold thread. She tried to see how it was done, but the wheel spun so fast it was all a blur. As she stared, her eyes began to feel heavy and soon she was fast asleep.

When she woke up, the little man had
vanished. But where the straw had been there
were now twenty neatly tied bundles of
glittering gold thread.

The key turned in the lock and the king
came into the room. He could barely believe his
eyes when he saw the gold. "You did it," he
gasped, clapping his hands in delight. Then he
began to think about all the things he could do
if he had even more gold.

So, the guard took the miller's daughter to another room. It was larger than the first, and filled with even more straw. Once more, he ordered her to turn the straw into gold overnight and once more, he locked her in.

No sooner had the key turned in the lock than the odd little man appeared from behind a mound of straw.

"I can help you," he said, stroking his beard. "But that's a lot of straw. It'll take me all night. What will you give me in return?"

"This ring on my finger is all I have left in the world," sighed the girl.

"I'll take it," he snapped. And he started spinning. Whirr, whirr, whirr went the wheel all night long. But, try as she might, the girl couldn't stay awake to see how it was done.

The next morning, the king was thrilled to find a hundred bundles of bright gold thread. But it only made him want more.

He led the miller's daughter to a third room. It was even bigger than the last, and it was crammed from floor to ceiling with straw.

"Being king is a costly business," he told her. "If you can spin all this, I'll have all the gold I'll ever need. And I'll make you my queen," he promised.

As soon as the girl was alone, the impish little man appeared again.

He took one look at the vast mound of straw and let out a whistle. "Now that's a lot of straw," he said. "I can help you," he said. "But it's a big job so it'll cost you."

"I have nothing left to give you," sobbed the miller's daughter.

"Well…" wheedled the little man. "It seems the king has taken a shine to you. If you become queen, then you must give me your first-born child."

The girl's mind was a whirl. She had no idea what might happen. So, reluctantly, she agreed. Satisfied with the deal, the little man set to his task once again.

Just as before, the miller's daughter fell asleep, but the little man worked furiously all night long. Whirr, whirr, whirr went the wheel,

faster and faster, as the little man raced against
the clock. Just as he finished spinning the last
bundle of golden thread, the key turned in
the lock, and he vanished.

The king flung open the door and was
dazzled by the great piles of gold that filled
the room. Then, standing in the midst of it all,
he set eyes on the miller's daughter.

Her hair shimmered like spun gold. For
the first time, the king noticed how stunningly
beautiful she was. He fell instantly in love
with her.

"I've been so caught up with greed, I've
treated you terribly," he cried. "If I promise
never to make you work at a spinning
wheel ever again, will you forgive me
and be my queen?"

The miller's daughter looked into his eyes
and saw that he meant every word. "I'd love to,"
was her happy reply.

They were married the very next day.
The king spared no expense on the celebrations.
He invited the old miller, the baker, and all
the other villagers to the castle, and the feasting
lasted long into the night.

It was the most lavish wedding
anyone in the kingdom could
remember. For once,
everyone agreed with the
miller when he boasted,
proudly, that his daughter
was the most beautiful
bride there had ever been.

The king and his new

queen were blissfully happy together. He was
a kind and generous husband, and she was
devoted to him.

The months passed, and the queen gave birth
to a beautiful son. She was so besotted with him
that she forgot all about promise she had made
to the strange little man.

Then, one dark winter's night, the queen was
rocking the baby to sleep when she felt an icy
breeze. She glanced up to see if the window
was open and gasped in horror.

There in front of her was the spindly little
man. "I've come to take what you owe me!"
he cried, and snatched the baby out of the cradle.

The queen was distraught. "I'll give you all
the riches of the kingdom, but please don't take
my baby!" she begged.

"Pah!" retorted the little man. "I can spin
all the gold and silver I'll ever want. Besides,
a promise is a promise."

The queen wept and pleaded with him, until
he couldn't take any more. "Very well,"
he snapped. "If you can guess my name in three
days, you may keep the child. If not, he will be
mine. I'll be back tomorrow, at midnight."

With that, he handed back the baby and vanished into the night.

All night and all the next day, the queen sat at her desk frantically scribbling out a list of all the names she had ever heard and some she wasn't even sure were real. Then she searched every book in the castle library for even more.

By nightfall, there were so many names on her list, the queen felt certain that the little man's name must be one of them.

At the stroke of midnight, he returned. "I'm back," he announced, with a mischievous chuckle. "So, can you guess my name?"

The queen unfolded her list. "Is your name, Caspar or Balthasar or Melchior?" she began.

But to each one, the little man shook his head and said, "That's not my name."

One by one, the queen read out every name on her list. But the man kept shaking his head more and more excitedly and repeating, "That's not my name, that's not my name!"

The queen reached the end of her list and sighed as the little man answered, "That's not my name," yet again. He laughed triumphantly. "Ha! You'll never guess it," he cried, and he vanished into the darkness.

But the queen was determined not to be beaten. The thought of losing her son was more than she could bear. So, the next day, she rode out to every village in the kingdom asking everyone their names and noting any new ones she came across.

That night, she came back to the castle with a list of the most outlandish names she had ever heard. "Surely, it must be one of these," she thought, hopefully.

At midnight, the little man appeared again. "Go on," he challenged her. "Guess my name."

The queen looked down at her new list. "Is your name Shortribs?" she asked.

The little man grinned and shook his head. "That's not my name," he giggled, "Guess again."

"Is your name Bandylegs?"

"That's not my name either," he chuckled, and his grin grew wider.

"Is it Crookedshanks?"

"That's not my name either," he chortled. "Not even close!" And his grin grew wider still.

By the time the queen had exhausted her list, she was distraught. She still hadn't guessed his name, and the little man was in fits of giggles.

On the third day, the queen rode out to all the most distant and desolate corners of the kingdom. But by the evening, she was desperate. She'd asked everyone she met for new names, but hadn't found a single one.

The heartbroken queen was about to return to the castle, when she spied a thin wisp of smoke rising above some trees.

She went closer to investigate, and there she saw a tiny cottage with a bonfire burning outside. To the queen's surprise, the peculiar little man himself was leaping around the fire, singing at the top of his voice. "The queen will never win this game, because Rumpelstiltskin is my name!" he warbled.

The queen wept for joy. "At last, I have his name!" she thought. And she raced home.

And so this time, when the little man appeared at midnight, he found the queen without a list. "So, do you give up?" he asked.

"Never!" retorted the queen. "Is your name Rrr...Robby?" she asked him first.

The man danced, gleefully, from one foot to the other. "That's not my name. Guess again," he laughed.

"Is your name Rrr...Ricky?" asked the queen

"That's not my name either," he crowed, leaping around the room.

The queen laughed. "Then just maybe... perhaps... could your name possibly be... Rrr...Rumpelstiltskin?" she asked.

The little man froze. His face turned from pink, to red, to deep, deep plum. "W-what? How did you find out?" he spluttered.

Rumpelstiltskin exploded
with rage. He stamped his foot
so hard that it went right into
the ground. Then, he stamped
his other foot even harder.

The angry little man
stomped and stamped himself
deep into the ground, right
up to his middle.

The deeper he went,
the angrier he became and
the angrier he was, the harder
he stomped.

Before long, Rumpelstiltskin
disappeared into the bowels
of the Earth, and he was
never seen again.

Tom Thumb

There was once an ordinary woodcutter and his wife who had an extraordinary son. He was no bigger than a man's thumb, but they loved him enormously. Because of his size, they named him Tom Thumb.

No matter how much his mother fed him, Tom never grew any taller. His parents were anxious that being so small might prevent him from doing the things other children did.

But Tom wasn't going to let his size get in the way of an adventure. He used a walnut shell as a canoe and a teaspoon as a paddle; he built himself a go-cart from a match box, with buttons for wheels; he even tamed a fieldmouse and made a little saddle for it so he could go out riding.

One morning, Tom Thumb's father was getting ready to go to work. "Please could you bring me the cart when you've finished with it?" he asked his wife.

"Mother's so busy," said Tom. "Why don't I bring it to you."

The woodcutter smiled at his son. "That's very kind of you, Tom, but you're far too small to lead a horse by the reins."

"That doesn't matter," said the boy. "I can sit in its ear and tell it which way to go."

"Very well," said the woodcutter. "Let's give it a try."

And so, when it was time to go, Tom's mother lifted him up into the horse's ear. "Giddy up!" he called, and the horse trotted obediently along the track.

They hadn't gone far, when they drove past two men from the circus, the ringmaster and a clown. The circus men were surprised to see a horse and cart go by without a driver. They were even more startled when the horse seemed to call out, "Giddy up!"

"I've never seen anything like it!" exclaimed the clown. "Was that a talking horse?"

"It must be some magic trick," said the ringmaster. "Let's follow and find out."

Tom Thumb drove on until he came to the spot where his father was working. "Here I am, Father," he called. "I've brought you the cart, just as I promised."

"Well done, Tom," said the woodcutter, holding out his hand next to the horse's ear.

Watching from behind a bush, the circus men could scarcely believe their eyes as they watched the tiniest boy they'd ever seen hop onto the palm of the woodcutter's hand.

"Did you see that?" asked the clown excitedly. "We'd make a fortune if we had that boy in our show."

The ringmaster rubbed his hands together greedily. "Yes, people would pay big money to see a boy that small," he agreed.

So the men strode over to the woodcutter. "Please allow us to introduce ourselves," began the ringmaster, with a theatrical bow. "We are performers from the circus. We couldn't help noticing that you have an unusually small son. He'd fit perfectly in our act."

"But, I don't–" began the woodcutter.

"Just think," the clown interrupted him. "With us, he could become a huge star, travel the world and see his name up in lights."

The ringmaster dug into his pocket and pulled out a bag of gold coins. "Of course, we'll make it worth your while," he said, jangling the coins.

"What? Sell my son?" cried the woodcutter.

"His mother and I wouldn't part with him for all the riches in the world."

But Tom sensed an opportunity. He climbed up his father's sleeve and whispered in his ear. "We really do need the money," he said. "Let me go with these jokers. I'll be back home before you know it – I promise."

The woodcutter couldn't help worrying about his son, but he knew he could take care of himself. So, he took the bag of gold and said goodbye to Tom.

With a satisfied smirk, the ringmaster put Tom on the brim of his top hat, and they set off.

They walked all afternoon, with Tom jigging along on the ringmaster's hat and whistling as he enjoyed the view. The light was starting to fade when they came to a crossroads. "Please may I get down for a moment?" Tom Thumb called. "I need to stretch my legs."

"Very well," said the ringmaster, setting the boy down at the side of the road.

"Thanks for the ride!" Tom called merrily, and he darted straight down a mouse hole.

"Hey, what do you think you're doing?" yelled the clown.

"Come out of there you little rascal," shouted the ringmaster, furiously.

The circus men poked twigs down the mouse hole, to try to force Tom out, but he just crawled further and further in, out of their reach.

By nightfall, the men had to admit defeat. "It's no use. We've lost him," the ringmaster sighed. "And all our gold, too!"

"I can't believe you fell for his trick," cried the clown. "You're meant to be the clever one."

"Well you didn't do much to help," retorted the ringmaster.

Tom listened to the two men bickering as they trudged home empty handed. He was just wondering what to do next, when a family of angry mice came and chased him out of the hole.

Outside, it was too dark for him to find his way home, so he looked around for somewhere to spend the night. He spotted an empty snail shell. "That will do nicely," he thought.

So, with some moss for a pillow and a leaf for a cover, he curled up

inside the shell. He was
just drifting off to
sleep, when he heard
voices overhead. So
he peered out to
see who it was.

A spotty youth,
clutching a big, bulging sack, was talking to
an older man. "Who are we going to rob next,
Dad?" asked the youth.

"There's a wealthy old priest who lives down
the road," his father replied. "Let's try him."

Tom was shocked. "I can't let these two
scoundrels rob a priest," he thought. So he got
out of the snail shell and followed them.

The robbers tiptoed around the priest's house
looking for a way to break in. "The doors have

got strong locks on them and there are iron bars on all of the windows," muttered the youth. "How are we going get in?"

"I'll help you!" Tom called up.

"Who's there?" whispered the youth.

"Where are you?" hissed the robber.

"I'm down here," Tom called.

The robbers looked down, stifling gasps of amazement. "What a tiny boy!" they exclaimed.

"My name's Tom Thumb," said the boy. "I can easily slip into the priest's house for you and get whatever you want."

"Well, you could certainly come in handy," agreed the robber. So he lifted Tom up onto the kitchen window ledge.

Tom slipped through the iron bars and jumped down onto the kitchen table. From there, he leaped onto a chair and slid down one of its legs to the floor. Then, at the top of his little lungs, he yelled, "I'm in the house. Now, what do you want me to steal?"

"Keep your voice down," hissed the robber through the window. "You'll wake everyone."

But, instead, Tom Thumb shouted even louder. "There are some fancy silver spoons here," he cried. "Do you want me to pass them out to you through the window?"

This time, the cook woke up. She sprang out of her bed and rushed to the kitchen, grabbing a rolling pin to fight off the intruder.

"Run!" cried the robber, and he and his son escaped into the night. Tom hurriedly climbed back up the chair and onto the table, but the window was too high for him to reach.

The cook looked around the room. "Who's there?" she called bravely. But she wasn't looking for a thumb-sized boy, so she didn't notice Tom, who quickly hid under a teacup. "I must have been dreaming," she thought, and she went back to bed.

Tom was so worn out from his adventures, that he curled up under the teacup and fell fast asleep. When he woke up it was morning. The cook was already up and busy in the kitchen.

Tom crawled out from under the teacup and looked for a way to escape. But, at that very moment, the kitchen cat looked up and spotted him.

Thinking Tom was a mouse, the cat sprang onto a chair and swiped a paw at the boy. Just in time, Tom ducked out of its way and hurled himself off the side of the table.

He had no choice but to run for the door. But, he was only half way across the room when a gigantic broom knocked him off his feet. The cook had started sweeping the floor. She swept Tom into a bucket full of scraps, which she carried to the yard and tipped out onto a heap of kitchen waste.

Tom fought his way out from under a pile of potato peelings, only to find himself nose-to-nose with a scavenging wolf. It stared at him hungrily and bared its razor-sharp teeth. Before Tom could dive out of the way, the wolf snapped him up and swallowed him, whole.

Sitting in the pit of the wolf's stomach Tom was surrounded by all sorts of disgusting things

Tom Thumb

the wolf had eaten. It gave him an idea. "Mister Wolf," he called. "It's me, the little boy you just ate."

"Be quiet," grumbled the wolf. "I'm trying to eat."

"I'm rather hungry myself," said Tom. "But I don't fancy any of the food here in your stomach. I know a place where you can feast on steaks, cheese and pies instead of scraps."

The wolf's mouth began to water. "Where is this place?" it asked greedily.

"I'll take you there," replied Tom. "Just follow my directions." He described the way back to his own house, and the wolf set off at a trot, driven by the thought of the delicious meal waiting at the other end.

When they reached his house, Tom directed the wolf to the back door and into the larder off the kitchen. Just as he'd promised, the shelves were stacked with meats and cheeses.

A freshly-baked pie was cooling on a rack, filling the room with the aroma of soft, buttery pastry. The wolf opened its jaws wide and was about to sink its teeth into the pie, when Tom Thumb began to howl with all his might.

"Stop that!" growled the wolf. "The owners of the house will hear."

But, of course, that was exactly what Tom Thumb wanted. So he kept on yelling until his parents came running.

When the woodcutter caught sight of the wolf, he grabbed his shot gun. "Stand back," he told his wife, and he took aim.

"Be careful, Father!" Tom shouted. "It's me, your son. The wolf has eaten me and I'm inside its stomach."

The woodcutter carefully lowered his gun, and the wolf tried to run past him. But, thinking fast, Tom's mother seized a frying pan from the stove. She beat the wolf over the head, and knocked it dead.

The woodcutter took out his hunting knife and carefully sliced open the beast's belly. Out hopped Tom Thumb.

"Tom, we've been so worried about you," his mother cried, stroking his hair with her little finger.

"Where have you been?" asked his father.

"It's been an incredible adventure," Tom Thumb began. "I've been down a mouse hole,

slept in a snail shell, foiled some robbers, been
chased by a cat and a broom, and eaten by
a greedy wolf. But I'm glad to be home and
I don't think I'll be going on any more
adventures for a long while."

Hansel and Gretel

Hansel and Gretel couldn't sleep. Their cruel stepmother had sent them to bed without any supper and their hungry tummies were rumbling loudly. Downstairs, they could hear raised voices.

"What will become of us?" they heard their father say. "We're down to our last loaf of bread. I can't afford to buy more food for the children."

"Never mind the children. We have to look after ourselves," snapped their stepmother. "Tomorrow we must take them into the forest and leave them there."

"We can't do that," their father protested. "The wild animals would tear them apart."

"Good riddance," their stepmother muttered under her breath. But aloud all she said was, "Nonsense! We can't survive on a woodcutter's wages. At least this way they stand a chance."

"I suppose you're right," he sighed.

When Gretel heard this, she began to sob. Hansel put his arm around his sister. "Don't cry," he said. "I've got an idea."

Hansel waited until he heard snoring from the next room. Then he put on his coat and tiptoed outside. The moon was shining brightly, making the pebbles gleam on the garden path. He stuffed as many as he could into his pockets and hurried upstairs.

The next morning, the children's stepmother woke them up very early. "Hurry up," she said sharply. "You must help us fetch firewood from the forest." She gave them each a small piece of

bread to take with them. "Don't eat it all at once," she warned.

As they walked through the forest, Hansel lagged behind. Every so often, when he was sure his stepmother wasn't looking, he dropped a pebble on the ground.

looking, he dropped a pebble on the ground.

They went deeper and deeper into the forest. Eventually, their father stopped. He gathered some sticks and made a fire to keep the children warm. "Wait here while we go and chop some wood," he said.

All morning long, Hansel and Gretel heard the comforting chop, chop, chop of their father's hatchet in the distance. "Maybe they've changed their minds," suggested Gretel hopefully.

Lunchtime came and went, but their father and stepmother didn't return. Hansel and Gretel were very hungry, but they nibbled their bread slowly to make it last.

As the afternoon wore on, it began to grow dark. The children added some sticks to the fire and lay down beside it. Before long, they were both fast asleep.

By the time the children woke up, the fire had died down. They could still hear the thud of the hatchet, but in the darkness the noise sounded sinister. Hansel shivered. "Let's go and look for them," he said.

They followed the sound, but found only the hatchet tied to a branch, swinging to and fro in the wind. "They've left us," whispered Gretel.

Hansel took his sister's hand. "Come with me," he said. "I've left a trail so we can find our way back." Sure enough, the white pebbles shone in the moonlight, showing them the way home.

It was morning by the time the children arrived at the cottage. They knocked at the door and their father answered it. He was delighted to see them safe.

But their stepmother was far from happy. That night, Hansel and Gretel overheard her nagging their father again. "We must get rid of those children or we'll all starve," she said. "What choice do we have?"

The woodcutter had no answer and so, reluctantly, he agreed to his wife's demands.

Hansel waited until they were asleep and sneaked downstairs to collect pebbles, just as before. But this time his stepmother was one step ahead of him. The door was locked.

He went back upstairs to Gretel. "Don't worry," he told her. "I'll think of something."

The next day, their father gave them each a piece of bread, and he and his wife took them into the forest once again.

Hansel broke his bread into tiny pieces. Every now and then, when no one was looking, he scattered a few crumbs on the ground.

This time, their stepmother led them even deeper into the forest. "I'll make sure they never find their way out," she said to herself.

As the woodcutter built a fire for his children, a tear rolled down his cheek. "Smoke in my eyes," he mumbled.

After their father and stepmother had gone, Gretel shared her bread with Hansel. Then they huddled together beside the fire for warmth. They were so tired that they soon dozed off.

When they woke up, only the red embers
of the fire were glowing and the daylight was
starting to fade. Hansel hunted around for
the trail of bread, but there was no sign of it.
"I'm sure it was around here," he said.

Just then, a snow-white bird flew down
and began pecking at something on the ground.
It was one of the pieces of bread that Hansel
had dropped. "Stop that!" he cried.

The bird was so startled that
it fluttered away, carrying its
prize in its beak.

Hansel ran to and fro,
searching for the rest of
his trail, but it was too
late. The hungry bird
had eaten it all.

"I think this is the way we came," said Gretel, pointing to a muddy track through the trees. The children followed it, but the forest soon became thicker and it was difficult to get through.

"I'm not sure this is right," said Hansel. They tried to turn back, but they couldn't find the way. Every direction looked the same.

On and on the children stumbled, all through the night and into the next morning. They wandered around in circles until they were completely lost. By this time they were so exhausted they could barely stand.

Then, just as they were ready to give up hope, the trees thinned out and they found themselves in a pretty forest glade. Hansel and Gretel stared in amazement. There before them was the most extraordinary little house they had ever seen.

It had gingerbread walls decorated with little sweets, and chocolate roof tiles dripping with sugary icing. Instead of flowers in the garden, there were scrumptious-looking cupcakes, giant lollipops and swirly candy canes.

There could hardly have been a more welcome sight for two hungry children.

Gretel ran up the path and licked one of the lollipops. "It's real!" she exclaimed.

"Let's eat some," said Hansel excitedly.

They nibbled the fence, munched through the window ledges and were just about to break off the door knocker and eat that too when the door swung open.

A gnarled old woman peered out at them. "Who are you?" she croaked. "Have you been eating my house?"

Hansel and Gretel nodded fearfully. With their cheeks stuffed with gingerbread, and chocolate all around their mouths, they could hardly deny it.

The old woman gave a toothless grimace. "Poor things. You must be ravenous," she said. "Come inside and you shall eat your fill."

She seemed harmless enough and the two children were still very hungry, so they followed her inside. But the moment they were through the door, she slammed it shut and locked it.

"Foolish brats," cackled the old woman. "You walked right into my trap."

Grabbing poor Hansel by the ear, she dragged him out to the chicken coop in the backyard and threw him inside. "You'll make a tasty supper once I've fattened you up!" she crowed.

The witch, for that was what she was, made Gretel work like a slave, preparing food for her brother. From morning until night, the girl peeled and chopped, boiled and stewed, roasted and baked, while the witch sat in a rocking chair counting jewels from her treasure chest.

After a week had gone by, the witch went out to the chicken coop. "Let me feel your plump little finger," she said to Hansel.

But Hansel was too clever for her. Instead of his finger, he poked an old chicken bone out through the bars.

The witch peered at the bone and prodded it.

"What a scrawny creature!" she exclaimed. Her eyesight was so poor that she couldn't tell the difference between a bone and a finger.

From then on, the witch made Gretel work

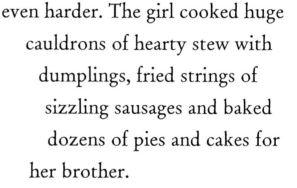

even harder. The girl cooked huge cauldrons of hearty stew with dumplings, fried strings of sizzling sausages and baked dozens of pies and cakes for her brother.

All this time, the witch sat greedily leafing through her books for tasty boy recipes. But, when she checked Hansel's finger at the end of the week, it was just as thin as before.

After a month had gone by, Hansel was still no chubbier. The witch, who was used to getting her way, finally lost her temper. "Today, I'm going to eat your brother, skinny or not," she said to Gretel. "Heat up the oven at once."

The witch followed Gretel's every move as the girl stoked up the fire. "Now get inside and check that it's starting to heat up," she said slyly, for secretly she planned to eat both the children.

But Gretel guessed what she was up to. "I can't fit in there," she declared.

"Of course you can, you silly goose," snapped the witch. "I'm much bigger than you and I can easily fit inside."

"Well, I really don't know how," said Gretel innocently. "You're much older and wiser than I am. Perhaps you could show me?"

With a snort of impatience, the witch pushed her aside and flung open the oven door. "Like this," she said, thrusting her head inside.

As quick as a flash, Gretel ran forward and gave her a big shove. Then she slammed the oven door and fastened it shut.

"Let me out!" shrieked the witch, banging on the door.

But Gretel didn't listen. She filled her pockets with jewels from the witch's treasure chest. Then she grabbed the key to the chicken coop and ran outside to rescue her brother.

"What's happening?" asked Hansel as Gretel opened the door.

"I've cooked the wicked witch," gasped Gretel. "Quickly, let's escape."

"But how will we find the way?" said Hansel.

At that moment, there was a rustle in the tree above. The children looked up and saw the bird that had eaten their bread.

It flew to the next tree and waited, with its head cocked. "I think it wants us to follow it," said Gretel.

So the children followed the bird through the forest until eventually they came to a stream with a rickety wooden bridge over it. "I know that bridge," said Hansel. "We're nearly home."

They thanked the bird and hurried off in the direction of their father's cottage. He was standing outside, and looked up when he heard them coming. "My children!" he cried.

They ran into his arms and he hugged them tightly. "I've missed you so much," he wept. "Please forgive me."

The three of them went inside. Hansel and Gretel looked around warily, but there was no sign of their stepmother.

"She left when the food ran out," their father explained. "There's not a crumb left in the house. I don't know how we'll manage, but I'll find a way," he promised.

"Perhaps these will help," said Gretel, emptying the witch's jewels out onto her lap.

"Where on earth did they come from?" asked Hansel in surprise.

Gretel tapped her finger on her nose. "You're not the only one with clever ideas, Hansel," she said with a smile.

The Twelve Dancing Princesses

There was once a king who had twelve beautiful and highly-spirited daughters. They loved singing and playing music and dressing up. But their real passion was dancing.

173

The princesses' mother had died soon after the youngest was born, so the king had brought them up on his own. They ran rings around him, and he always gave them everything they wanted.

But recently, the princesses weren't as lively as usual. They barely said a word in their public speaking classes, and they yawned all the way through a dinner for a visiting ambassador.

The king didn't know what to do. "It's probably just a phase," he thought. "They'll grow out of it."

Then, one morning, he received an enormous bill from the royal shoemaker for twelve dozen pairs of dancing shoes.

"This won't do!" exclaimed the king.

He summoned the princesses to his study. "I've been too soft on you girls," he told them, "From now on, I want you to focus on your royal duties. That means there will be no more late nights, no more parties and absolutely no more dancing."

To the king's surprise, the princesses didn't argue, not even the eldest, who usually had an answer to everything. But, as they shuffled out of his study, he heard a muffled giggle. "They're up to something," he thought.

That night, the king sent the princesses to their bedroom early and locked the door. "It's for their own good," he reassured himself. "I don't want them coming to any harm."

In the morning, when the maid went to wake the princesses, she tripped over a pile of dancing shoes that had been left out in the hallway. The shoes were battered and their soles were worn right through. The maid hurried off to tell the king.

"Those girls have been out dancing," the king complained. "But how?" The princesses' bedroom was at the top of a tall tower with only one door. "They must have climbed out of a window," thought the king. He called the princesses to his study, but they refused to say where they had been.

So, that night, he sent his daughters to bed early again. This time, he bolted all the windows as well as locking the door. "There won't be any dancing tonight," he said confidently.

But the next morning, the maid found another pile of ruined dancing shoes.

The Twelve Dancing Princesses

Again, the princesses refused to say what they'd been up to. The king groaned. "Someone must have let them out," he said.

So, that night, he sent his daughters to bed early again. This time, he bolted the windows, locked the door *and* ordered guards to stand watch. "That should stop them from going anywhere," said the king. But it didn't.

The princesses still wouldn't tell the king their secret. So, the next night, he stood watch with the guards. He didn't see or hear a thing all night. But, in the morning, there was yet another pile of ragged shoes.

No matter what the king tried, the princesses still managed to go out dancing every night. His shoe bill grew longer, and his temper grew shorter.

The king had run out of ideas. So he made an announcement. "Any man who can come to the palace and find out where my daughters go dancing every night, may choose one of them for his wife," he decreed. "But if he fails, he must pay my shoe bill," he added.

It wasn't long before a young prince came to the palace to take up the king's challenge. "It should be easy," he boasted. "All I have to do is stay awake all night and follow the princesses to wherever they go."

"That's what you think," thought the eldest princess. When it was time for bed, she led the prince to a small guest room next to the bedroom where she and her sisters slept. Then, she brought him a steaming cup of creamy hot chocolate.

"Please, make yourself at home," she said with a charming smile. "I've put some extra soft pillows on the bed for you."

The prince sat on the bed and sipped his hot chocolate. He didn't mean to fall asleep, but the bed was very comfortable, and his eyelids soon grew heavy.

The eldest princess giggled. "He won't be spoiling our fun tonight," she told the others. "I've put a sleeping potion in his drink."

The next thing the prince knew, it was morning and the maid was shaking him awake. Out in the hallway was a pile of tattered shoes.

The king wasn't impressed when he heard that the prince had slept through everything. He called for his guards. "Take this useless boy away!" he ordered.

Months passed. Many other princes came, each more confident than the last. But they all failed to solve the mystery.

The king grew more and more frustrated. "These princes are hopeless," he sighed. "I wish someone would come and put an end to all this nonsense."

It just so happened that the next day, a poor soldier arrived in the kingdom. He had heard about the king's challenge and decided to try his luck. He was striding through the forest to the palace, when he came across an old woman.

"Young man," she called in a wavering voice. "Please help a poor, starving old woman."

The soldier felt sorry for the old woman. So, although he was poor and hungry himself, he gave her what little food he had.

The old woman thanked him eagerly.
"In return for your kindness, I'd like to give you
a small gift," she said. She dug into her bag and
pulled out a cloak that was as light as a cobweb.
"Try it on," she said, handing it to the soldier.

To the soldier's amazement, as soon as
he pulled the cloak around his shoulders,
he disappeared. And when he took it off again,
he reappeared. "An invisibility cloak!" he cried.
"With this I'll surely be able to solve the
mystery of the twelve dancing princesses."

He turned to thank the old woman, but she had vanished. So he packed the cloak carefully into his bag and set off for the palace.

When the soldier arrived at the palace, the king invited him to join them for dinner. "There's something different about this young man," thought the king. "I hope he succeeds."

Over dinner, the soldier told the princesses about his adventures in the army and they entertained him with stories of their own. He gazed around the table. Each princess was lovelier than the last. The youngest princess smiled sweetly at the soldier and blushed. "She's the loveliest of all," he thought.

When it was time for bed, the eldest princesses showed the soldier to his room and brought him a cup of hot chocolate. He was

about to take a sip, when he noticed
the youngest princess watching anxiously.
"Perhaps I shouldn't drink this," he thought.

So, when no one was looking, the soldier
poured the hot chocolate into a plant pot.
He yawned loudly, lay down and pretended
to snore.

He listened to the princesses whispering next
door. "The soldier's nice," said the youngest.
"But I don't think he can afford to pay for our
shoes. Maybe we shouldn't go out tonight."

"And miss our fun?" cried the others.

"Don't be so soft," teased the eldest princess.
"Now hurry up and put on your dancing shoes."

The soldier heard more excited whispering,
tiptoed footsteps and a rustling of skirts. Then
all fell silent.

He threw on his magic cloak and crept into the princesses' bedroom. It was empty. But, in the middle of the room, a rug had been rolled back to reveal a secret staircase.

The soldier hurried down the stairs. But in his haste to catch up with the princesses, he accidentally trod on the youngest one's dress.

"Oh," she squealed. "Someone pulled my dress."

The eldest princess looked back. "Don't be silly," she said. "There's no one there. You must have caught it on a nail."

At the bottom of the stairs, a door opened out into a magical underground park. To the soldier's astonishment, the trees sparkled with silver leaves frosted with diamonds.

The soldier had never seen anything like it. He reached out and broke off a glittering twig to take back with him. It made a loud crack.

The youngest princess jumped. "Did you hear that?" she asked her sisters. "I'm sure we're being followed."

"Don't be silly," the eldest princess scolded her. "It must have been the fireworks from the castle," she said, pointing ahead.

There, in front of them, a lake gleamed in the moonlight. On the far side stood a splendid, inviting castle. The sky was ablaze with fireworks that were reflected on the water like a million shimmering jewels.

At the shore there were twelve little boats. A handsome prince was waiting in each one, ready to row the princesses across to the castle.

The princesses skipped down to the water's edge and stepped into their boats. The soldier sneaked into the boat with the youngest princess. It rocked dangerously as he sat next to her.

"There's something strange going on tonight," said the princess, as the prince rowing her boat struggled to keep up with the others. But her sisters weren't listening.

When they reached the other side, the princes tied up their boats, and lifted the princesses onto the shore. Two by two, the twelve couples entered the castle with the invisible soldier following close behind.

A pair of grand, mirrored doors opened before them. Inside, was a magnificent ballroom lined with vast, golden mirrors and lit by enormous crystal chandeliers.

The moment they stepped through the doors, the room was suddenly filled with beautiful, lilting music. The music swelled, and they began to dance, twirling gracefully as though they were under its spell.

As they glided across the polished marble floor, each princess looked more stunning than the last. But the soldier only had eyes for the youngest. Her hair shone, her eyes sparkled and her dainty feet scarcely touched the ground.

"I wish *I* was dancing with her," he thought.

The twelve princesses danced until their shoes were worn right through. Then, just as suddenly as it had begun, the music stopped. They reluctantly returned to their boats, and the princes rowed them back across the lake.

As before, the soldier rode in the boat with
the youngest princess. When they reached
the other side, he leaped ashore and raced ahead.
He jumped into his bed, just as the princesses
arrived home.

Tired but happy, the princesses kicked off
their ruined shoes. Then, they looked in on
the soldier, who pretended to snore loudly.

"He's been asleep all night," said the eldest
princess. "I told you there was nothing to
worry about."

"He's nice," said the youngest thoughtfully.
"I wish we hadn't tricked him."

Under his bed covers, the soldier smiled as he
heard the princesses tiptoe into their bedroom
and close the door. He couldn't wait
for the morning.

The princesses
hadn't been asleep
for long when the
maid came to wake
them. She unlocked the
tower door to find the usual pile
of tattered dancing shoes out in
the hallway. But, to her surprise,
she also found the soldier wide awake.

The soldier rushed excitedly to the king's
study and the twelve princesses shuffled in
behind him, yawning and bleary-eyed.

"Well?" asked the king.

"Your Majesty," the soldier said cheerfully.
"I've solved the mystery for you."

"Really?" asked the king, raising
a questioning eyebrow.

"Yes," answered the soldier. "I know where the twelve princesses go every night." He told the king all about his magic cloak, the secret staircase, the glittering trees and the enchanted castle across the shimmering lake.

The king wasn't convinced. "How can I be sure you're telling the truth?" he asked warily.

The soldier pulled out his silver twig. "I brought back proof!"

Now the king was convinced. "So, what do you have to say for yourselves?" he asked his daughters. The princesses hung their heads guiltily, but said nothing.

The youngest blushed. "It's all true," she finally blurted out. "Please forgive us."

The king turned to the soldier. "You have solved the mystery," he said. "Now you may claim your reward. Which of my twelve daughters would you like to marry?"

This time, the soldier blushed. "The youngest and sweetest," he answered. "If she'll have me."

"I will!" was her happy reply.

"Then we must throw a party of our own," the king announced.

And so everyone in the kingdom was invited to the palace for a grand ball. The princesses and their guests danced all night.

And the king danced most of all.

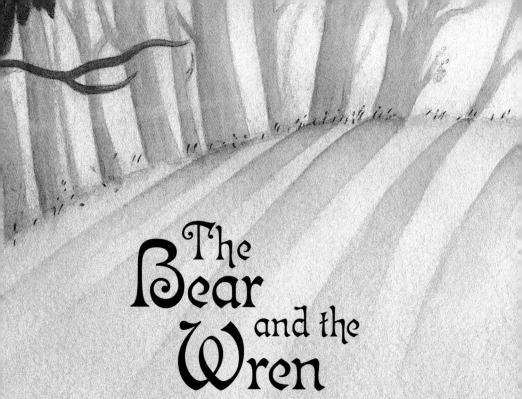

The Bear and the Wren

One spring morning, a bear and a wolf were walking in the forest. Sunlight slanted through the trees and birdsong floated on the breeze.

The bear had never heard such lovely music in his life. "Who is singing that beautiful tune?" he asked.

"That, my friend, is the king of the forest," replied the wolf.

The bear was surprised. "I didn't even know there was a king of the forest," he said. "I wonder where his palace is."

In fact, the bird that was singing wasn't a king at all, but a perfectly ordinary little wren. A short while later, the wren flew past, with a worm in his beak, and disappeared among the branches of a tree.

The wolf and the bear crept over to the tree and stared up. "The king's palace must be up there," said the bear. "I'd love to see it."

The eager bear started to climb the tree, but

the wolf caught him by the tail. "Not so fast," he said. "Wait for the king to go out again."

The bear paced impatiently around the tree until the wren finally flew off, and then he clambered up. But when he reached the nest, he was disappointed to see that the king's palace was nothing but a hole in the tree trunk, stuffed with moss. Worse still, the chicks were just scraps of brown fluff with bulging black eyes and gaping yellow beaks.

"What ugly creatures!" he exclaimed. "You can't be princes and princesses, and this pathetic nest certainly isn't fit for a king."

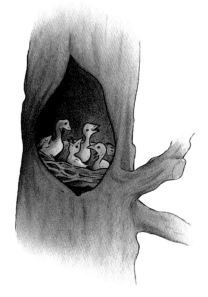

"How dare you be so rude?" the chicks cheeped.

"Father will make you pay for this."

The bear was unconcerned. He simply shrugged and slid back down the tree.

The chicks squawked angrily until their father returned to the nest. "That big brown bear said we were ugly," they told him.

The wren ruffled his feathers and puffed out his chest. "I'll teach him a lesson," he said. He flew straight to the cave where the bear was sleeping and pecked him on the snout.

The bear woke with a start. "Ouch! That hurt," he growled.

"What gives you the right to insult my family?" cried the wren. "This is war!"

"If you insist," replied the bear sleepily. "We'll do battle tomorrow. But I don't see how a puny wren can possibly beat me."

"I'll show you," the wren retorted. And he flew off to gather his troops.

All the four-legged animals in the forest took sides with the bear, while an army of winged creatures joined the wren.

That night, the wren sent a fly to spy on the animals. The fly hid inside a flower and listened in as the bear spoke.

"Fox, you're the most cunning of us all," he said. "What's your battle plan?"

"We need a secret signal," the fox replied. "When I raise my tail, that's the order to charge; if I let it hang down, run away as fast as you can."

The fly reported back to the wren, who hatched a cunning plan of his own. He gathered a team of wasps and gave them a special mission.

At dawn, the forest rang with battle cries
from both sides, as the two armies lined up to
face one another. On one side, wolves howled
and bears roared, and four-legged animals of
all shapes and sizes pounded the earth with
a thunderous drumming of hooves and paws.

In the air, the winged army of screeching
birds and buzzing insects hovered like a heavy
storm cloud about to break.

When the fox raised his bushy tail,
the animals charged, and the winged
creatures swooped down to meet them.

At the wren's signal, one of the wasps dived under the fox's tail. It stung him fiercely, but the brave fox kept his tail in the air.

So the wren sent down another wasp. The fox yelped in pain, but still he managed to keep his tail up.

When a third wasp stung him, the fox couldn't take any more. He pulled down his tail between his legs, whimpering with pain.

As soon as they saw this, the animals turned and fled the battlefield. The clever little wren and his winged army had won.

Singing triumphantly, the wren flew home to his chicks. "We have beaten the bear," he announced proudly. "He'll think twice before insulting us again."

But the chicks weren't satisfied. "He still owes us an apology," they cheeped. The wren agreed, so he sent a messenger to bring the bear back to the nest.

Anxious to avoid another humiliating defeat, the bear came immediately. He bowed down at the foot of the tree. "Please forgive

me," he called up humbly. " I should never
have been rude to you."

"We forgive you," agreed the wren, "as long
as you promise to be polite to my family and
to accept me as your king."

"I promise," said the bear solemnly.

So the bear and the wren made their peace,
and the animals, birds and insects gathered at
the heart of the forest to celebrate. They ate,
drank and had a merry time together.

And, from that day on, they
all agreed that the wren
really was the king of
the forest.

King Thrushbeard

The king groaned as his daughter turned down yet another handsome prince. He had invited all the suitable young men from miles around to meet the princess, but so far she had found fault with each of them.

The first was rather pale. "He's as white as a ghost," complained the princess, who always spoke her mind. The next had a ruddy complexion. "Tomato face," she mocked. Another was tall and lanky. "Skinny as a bean pole," she said. She called the fourth, "a wrinkled prune," because he was older than the rest.

One by one, every man was sent away feeling scorned and dejected. When the last suitor stepped up to the throne, the princess hooted with laughter. "Look at his pointed beard. It's just like a thrush's beak," she said. "I couldn't possibly marry him!" And from then on, everybody called him King Thrushbeard.

The king was outraged at his daughter's rudeness. "You'll never find a better match than that last king." he said. "He's a charming young man, and he rules a vast kingdom. But since you refuse to behave like a princess and treat people kindly, I'll have you marry the next beggar that comes along," he exclaimed.

That afternoon, a poor fiddler came to the palace, hoping to earn a few pennies. The king called the man inside to play for him and the princess.

The fiddler's clothes were old and ragged, but the music he played was sweet and soulful. When he had finished, he politely asked the king for a small reward.

"I enjoyed your music so much, I'll give you more than a few pennies," the king declared. "I'll give you my daughter's hand in marriage."

"You can't make me marry that wretch," protested the princess. But no matter how much she complained, the king was determined to keep his oath. He called for a priest immediately, and they were married right there and then.

As soon as the ceremony was over, the king turned to his daughter. "My palace is no place for a beggar-woman," he said. "You must go now and live with your husband."

And so the fiddler led the princess away from the palace. Before long, they came to a forest the princess had never seen before. "Who owns this beautiful forest?" she asked.

"This is King Thrushbeard's hunting forest," he replied.

"If only I'd accepted his proposal," she sighed.

Further along the road, they passed a meadow, where cows were grazing contentedly. "Whose pretty meadow is this?" she asked.

"It's King Thrushbeard's," came the reply.

The princess sighed again, "If only I hadn't turned him down."

A while later, they came to a city with grand buildings and wide streets bustling with wealthy merchants. "Who rules this splendid city?" the princess asked the fiddler.

"King Thrushbeard, of course," he answered.

"If only I had agreed to marry him," said the princess, "all this would have been mine."

At this, the fiddler turned to the princess with a wounded expression. "Don't you realize how much it hurts me to hear you saying that you wish you'd married someone else?" he said sadly. "Don't you think I'm good enough?"

He seemed so upset that, for once, the princess wished she hadn't said anything.

They walked on in silence, until they came to a tiny wreck of a hut. "Who can live in such a miserable little house?" asked the princess.

"I do," answered the fiddler proudly, "and now you do too." He held open the door for her, and she blushed as she stooped to go inside.

The princess looked around the one room curiously and asked, "Where are the servants?"

"There aren't any," replied the fiddler. "You'll have to do all the work around the house yourself. Why don't you start by lighting the stove and cooking us some dinner? I'm starving after our journey."

But the princess had never done any kind of housework before. She broke one of her immaculately manicured nails trying to light the stove and refused to do any more. Eventually the fiddler had to step in and help.

The next morning, the fiddler woke her up before dawn. "I'm going out," he said. "You'd better wash last night's dishes, then you can get on with cleaning the house, weeding the vegetable patch and making dinner."

Alone in the house,
the princess thought, "If only I
hadn't been so fussy, I wouldn't
be living in this hovel." But, since
she had nowhere else to go, she had
no choice but to make the best of it.

It wasn't easy. Doing the dishes,
she spilled soap suds everywhere.
In the garden, she fell in a patch of
stinging nettles. She cried over
the onions and cut her finger
chopping the carrots.

When the fiddler came home,
he found the princess staring at the burned
remains of a stew through floods of tears.
"Don't cry," he said softly. "Here, let me help
you." And together they made a fresh stew.

For a few weeks, they got by with what little they had. The princess struggled to get used to her new life, but the fiddler was so kind and caring that she grew fond of him. "He may be a beggar," she thought, "but he has a good heart and a handsome face."

One day, they opened the larder to find there was practically nothing left to eat. All they had was a rotting potato, a few limp cabbage leaves and a scrap of bacon. The princess boiled them up to make a watery soup.

"We can't live like this any longer," said the fiddler. "You're going to have to find a way to earn some money. Perhaps you could weave willow baskets to sell," he suggested. The princess was eager to help, but every basket she tried to weave fell apart in her lap.

"Never mind, perhaps you'll be better at spinning," said the fiddler. So he borrowed a spinning wheel. The princess tried her best, but the coarse thread cut her soft fingers and she bled all over the wool.

"It's no use," said the fiddler. "You'll have to sell my mother's old china at the market." And he took down all the cups and plates from the dresser and piled them into a box.

"What if people from my father's kingdom see me selling dishes in the street," thought the princess. "It will be so humiliating."

But she swallowed her pride and went to the market. Before she had sold a thing, a drunken horseman came galloping up the road, out of control. He crashed into the princess's stall, smashing everything to smithereens.

"Our china! It's ruined and I haven't got
a penny. What are we going to live off now?"
wailed the princess, and she ran home to tell
her husband what had happened.

The fiddler comforted her. "Don't worry,"
he said. "I'll go to the palace and ask King
Thrushbeard if there's any work you can do
for him there."

And so the princess found herself
working as a kitchen maid. From dawn
to dusk, she peeled and chopped
vegetables, washed dishes and
scrubbed floors. It was hard
work, but she was allowed to
take home any leftover food,
so she and the fiddler never
went hungry.

Then, one day, the cook announced that they had a special feast to prepare. King Thrushbeard was going to celebrate his marriage. The kitchen buzzed with excitement and curiosity. "Who is his mystery bride?" everyone wondered.

All week, delivery boys arrived at the kitchen laden with baskets of tropical fruit and fresh vegetables, herbs and exotic spices, huge cheeses, succulent meats, cases of fine wine and barrels of foaming ale. The princess was run off her feet unloading the deliveries and helping the cook.

In the past, the princess would have spent the week before a party planning her outfit and deciding which jewels went with her dress. Now, she was so busy she didn't have time to think about how much her life had changed, or to feel sorry for herself.

When the day of
the wedding came, the fiddler
told the princess, "Make sure
you get a good view so you can tell me all
about it later."

So, as the guests trooped in, all bringing
wedding gifts, she hid behind a pillar to watch
the festivities.

Servants streamed past her carrying dishes
piled high with party food. Now and then, they
would stop to give her a few morsels, which she
put in her pockets to take home to the fiddler.

A gong was sounded and King Thrushbeard
entered the hall. Dressed in a blue velvet coat,
he was incredibly handsome. His neatly trimmed
beard didn't look ridiculous at all. In fact, it
made him look so distinguished that the princess

wondered how she could ever have mocked him for his looks.

She looked on as the king walked through the hall, greeting his admiring guests. But, then, to her dismay, he caught her eye. She drew back behind the pillar, hoping he wouldn't recognize her, but it was too late.

The king strode over to her and took her by the hand. "Please, come and dance with me," he said, leading her into the middle of the hall. The princess panicked, but as she tried to pull away, the scraps of food spilled from her pockets all over the floor.

With the guests' laughter ringing in her ears and tears of humiliation welling in her eyes, the princess wished the ground could swallow her up. She turned and fled.

King Thrushbeard went after her and caught up with her in the corridor. The princess bowed her head in shame. "I'm sorry I've spoiled your wedding party."

"Don't worry," answered a familiar voice. "You haven't spoiled anything"

The princess looked up, confused. There, smiling at her was her husband, the fiddler, dressed in King Thrushbeard's clothes.

"I don't understand," she gasped. "Are you the king, or the fiddler?"

"I'm both," replied King Thrushbeard. "I've loved you since I first set eyes on you, but you weren't interested. So I disguised myself as a poor fiddler to teach you to be humble," he explained. "I'm sorry I tricked you, but I hope that you've learned to love me too."

The princess smiled. "I have," she said.
"And I promise to treat people with
kindness and respect from now on – no
matter who they are or what they look like."

"In that case," said the king, "we have
a wedding to celebrate." He clapped his hands
and a team of maids whisked away the princess
and dressed her in a silk robe, a gold tiara and
satin shoes.

With her transformation complete,
the princess linked arms with the king, and they
returned to the hall amid great whoops and
cheers from the guests.

Then King Thrushbeard picked up his
precious fiddle. He played a jolly jig
and led the entire party in a dance
all around the palace.

The princess soon settled into her new life as Queen Thrushbeard and was happier than she'd ever been before.

True to her promise, she never said a bad word about anyone ever again. She apologized to all the suitors she'd so rudely rejected, and even helped them to find princesses of their own to marry.

The Goose Girl

The princess sighed as she took one last look around her bedroom. She was getting married to a young king from a kingdom far away, and it was time for her to leave her childhood home.

Outside, a maid was already sitting astride a sturdy brown mare, and the queen was saddling up her silver stallion, Falada, for the princess to ride.

Putting on a brave smile, the princess went downstairs. "Well, Mother, I'm all packed and ready to go," she said to the queen, with a mix of sadness and excitement.

The queen kissed her daughter on the forehead. "Go safely," she told her. "Stay with Falada, and he will look after you."

"I will," said the princess tearfully, and she climbed onto the horse.

Falada was no ordinary horse. He was noble and dignified and, when there was something important to be said, he could talk. The queen trusted him above any of her advisers.

She stroked his velvety nose and whispered in his ear, "Please take care of the princess for me."

The horse bowed his head and answered softly, "I will, Your Majesty." Then, he proudly tossed his mane, and they set off.

As they rode away, the princess turned and waved. "Goodbye, Mother," she called. She kept on waving until the castle disappeared into the distance.

Then, she turned to gaze at the road ahead and began to daydream about the new life that was waiting for her.

After few miles, they came to a stream. The water looked cool and refreshing, so the Princess asked the maid, "Please could you get me a drink of water from that stream?"

But the maid didn't budge. "If you want a drink, you can get it yourself," she snapped. "I didn't ask to be your maid."

The princess was shocked. No maid had ever been so rude to her. But she didn't want to argue, so she jumped down from Falada and went to the stream to drink.

She leaned over to scoop up some water. But she lost her balance and fell into the stream with a splash. She watched in dismay as her gold crown was swept away.

The maid laughed as the princess struggled to her feet, shivering and bedraggled.

Falada swished his tail angrily. "Can't you see the princess is cold? Give her your cloak at once," he ordered the maid.

This time, the maid did as she was told.

The Goose Girl

"If the horse can talk," she thought, "who knows what other powers it might have."

Back on the road, the princess soon forgot about the maid's disobedience and started thinking about her wedding. After a while, they came to another stream. "Please could you get me a drink of water?" she asked the maid.

But the maid simply stuck her nose in the air. "If you want a drink, get it yourself," she replied again. "I didn't ask to be your maid."

As before, the princess didn't want to argue. But this time when she went to drink, she took great care not to land in the water again.

Once she had drunk her fill, the princess turned to get back on her horse, but the maid stood in her way. "My saddle's so hard and lumpy, I'm covered in bruises," complained the maid. "Can't we switch horses for a few miles?"

"Oh, you poor thing," said the princess. "Falada, please take the maid for a while."

The stallion snorted uneasily as the maid yanked his mane and heaved herself onto his saddle, but he did as the princess asked.

They rode on all day, along winding rivers, up steep, rocky mountains and through shady forests. The sun was beginning to set when they finally arrived at the king's palace.

The king and an excited crowd of courtiers rushed out to greet them. The princess had lost her crown, her hair was a mess and she was still wearing the maid's tatty brown cloak. Riding high on Falada, and wearing a haughty expression, the maid looked far more majestic.

The royal party gathered around the maid, thinking she was the king's bride. Sweeping her up in his arms, the king carried her inside.

The real princess tried to follow them, but she was stopped by a guard.

"Please let me in. There's been a silly mistake," she told him. "I'm the princess. That girl with the king is only a maid."

"You should see the state you're in," said the guard, mockingly. "You're obviously no princess." And he stubbornly refused to let her through.

Meanwhile, the maid was led to an elegant banqueting hall where the table was laid with a sumptuous meal.

"This is the life," she thought smugly, as she took her seat. "I never wanted to be a servant, and now these people think I'm a princess!"

Sitting opposite her, the king was puzzled. She didn't look much like a princess to him. But he pushed his doubts aside. "She must just be tired after her long journey," he thought.

After dinner, a band began to play, and the king took the maid by the hand for a dance. While the other guests twirled gracefully around the room, she jigged and hopped from one foot to the other. "She's rather ungainly for a princess," he thought. "But maybe that's the way they dance where she comes from."

When the music stopped, they went out onto the balcony for some air. Below them, the palace gardens were bathed in pale moonlight, and the stars twinkled brightly above.

It should have been a magical evening, but the king felt uneasy somehow. Then, he caught sight of the real princess, who was standing at the stable door, stroking Falada's mane.

"Isn't that the girl who rode here with you?" he asked the maid. "Would you like me to send someone down to show her to the servants' sleeping quarters?"

"Oh no, she's just a peasant. I brought her along to carry my bags," said the maid. "I don't know why she's still hanging around. Perhaps you could give her some work digging the fields to keep her out of the way – I mean busy."

The king looked down at the princess. She was so delicately beautiful, she didn't look much like a peasant to him. He didn't like to think of her digging the fields. So he said, "I have a young boy who looks after the geese. She can help him."

"Ha! That's the princess dealt with," thought the maid. "Now I'd better make sure that talking horse doesn't give me away."

So, the next morning, the maid called for the local butcher. "That horse I rode here was terribly dangerous. The beast threw me off several times," she said. "I want you to destroy it at once."

"Certainly," said the butcher.

Out in the stables, he found the princess with Falada. She was horrified when he told her his orders. "Please don't kill my horse," she begged, flinging her arms around Falada's neck.

"I don't see why I should listen to a peasant girl instead of the king's bride," retorted the butcher.

"But I'm a pri—" she began, and then she stopped, realizing that he'd never believe her. "I promise I'll make it up to you as soon as I can," she said solemnly.

She was so lovely, he couldn't find it in his heart to refuse. "All right, then," he replied gruffly. "But you'll have to keep the horse outside the town wall, so no one finds out."

And so, the princess began her new life as a goose girl, while the maid settled into hers in the palace, where she made the servants' lives miserable. One day, she deliberately walked her muddy shoes all over the cream carpet they had just cleaned. The next day, she demanded a complicated ten-course meal, then sent most of the food back, untouched. She never once said please or thank you. In next to no time, she had made herself thoroughly unpopular.

The princess decided to stay out of the maid's way, until she could prove who she really was. Early every morning, she and the goose boy herded the king's geese out of the palace yard. The geese waddled and waggled their way through a gateway in the town wall to a lush green meadow beyond, where the Princess kept Falada safe from view.

Whenever the goose boy was out of earshot, the princess would nuzzle Falada and talk to him softly.

"This is no life for us, Falada," she said to him one morning. "You should be galloping free, not hiding out here, and I should be planning my wedding to the king."

The horse tossed his mane proudly. "Trust me, Princess," he replied. "I will make sure that the king hears the truth."

Comforted by Falada's words, she sat down on the grass, and began to comb her long, golden hair. The goose boy stared in fascination as it tumbled down her shoulders. He desperately wanted to touch it, so he reached out a little, grubby hand.

Falada whinnied indignantly, and the princess looked up. When she saw what the boy was about to do, she chanted, "Gentle wind, blow this way and that. Blow away this rascal's hat."

The wind immediately whirled
around the boy, snatching his hat off
and playfully tossing it on the breeze. "Hey,
that's not fair!" cried the boy, as he chased across
the meadow after it.

The same thing happened the next day, and
the day after that. Day after day, the goose boy
would try to touch the princess's golden hair
only for her to call up the wind, sending him
chasing after his hat again.

The goose boy grew more and more frustrated, until he decided he'd had enough. He went to see the king. "Please, Your Majesty," he began nervously. "I don't want that girl to look after the geese with me any more."

"Why ever not?" asked the king.

"Because she teases me all day long with her tricks," the goose boy complained.

"What sort of tricks?" asked the king curiously.

The goose boy told the king how the girl was able to command the wind. "I think she might be a witch," he said.

"If what you say is true, then there's certainly something special about her," replied the king. "But if you take her out with you just one more time, I'll let you look after the geese on your own again after that."

The next morning, the king woke up early.
He disguised himself in a hooded cloak. Then,
he followed the goose boy and the princess out
of the palace yard, lurking in the shadows so
they wouldn't notice him. While they herded
the geese into the meadow, he hid in the gateway
behind them and watched.

As usual, the princess waited until the goose
boy was out of earshot, then she spoke to Falada.
"The royal wedding is tomorrow," she said sadly.
"How am I ever going to stop the king from
marrying that dreadful maid?"

Falada's nose twitched and he pricked up
his ears. Looking over the princess's shoulder,
he spotted the cloaked figure in the gateway.
Despite the disguise, he recognized the king
at once.

The Goose Girl

"We will prove that you are the king's true bride," said Falada, raising his voice to make sure the king could hear. "Trust me, you'll have your perfect wedding," he promised.

The king could scarcely believe his ears. He had never heard a horse talk before. "Can this extraordinary creature be telling the truth?" he wondered.

He watched as the princess combed her hair. It shone like the sun, and he was utterly bedazzled. When the goose boy tried to touch it, the king was astonished to see her call up the wind, just as the boy had described.

That was all the proof the king needed. "No ordinary peasant can command the wind. She must be my true bride," he thought, and he hurried home, determined to put things right.

That evening, the king summoned all his courtiers and all his servants to the palace, including the goose boy and the princess. When everyone had gathered in the throne room, he announced that he had a curious tale to tell.

Naming no names, he told them the story of a princess whose maid had forced her to switch places with her. Then, he turned to the princess, "Tell me, if you were the princess, how would you punish the maid?" he asked.

The princess blushed and glanced warily at the maid. "If she said she was sorry and promised to be good in the future, that would be enough for me," she replied.

"What?" scoffed the maid. "If it was my maid, I'd throw her in a barrel of nails and roll it through the town until she was dead!"

"So that's how you would punish yourself is it?" asked the king. "The maid in my story is you, and this goose girl is the real princess."

"What nonsense! I'm a pri–" the maid began, but she stopped, seeing that no one believed her. "Don't throw me in a barrel. I didn't mean it!"

"I could never inflict such a cruel punishment on anyone," said the king. "But will you apologize to the princess?"

"Never," she retorted haughtily. She shoved the princess and the goose boy out of her way and ran for the door.

"Guards! Seize her," ordered the king. And the maid was dragged back to the king, kicking and screaming.

"Since you refuse to apologize," said the king, "your punishment will be to do all the dirtiest jobs. I want you to dig the fields, muck out the stables and clean all the carpets."

The maid grumbled as the guards took her away, but no one paid her the slightest notice.

All eyes were on the princess. "How did you find out the truth?" she asked the king.

"I had my suspicions," he replied. "But it was the goose boy and your talking horse who convinced me."

The royal wedding went
ahead the next day. At the princess's
request, a few extra guests were invited –
Falada and the goose boy were her page boys,
and a whole gaggle of geese waddled down the
aisle behind her as her bridesmaids.

It was the perfect wedding the princess
had hoped for, and it was clear to everyone
there that the king and his true bride were
going to be very happy together.

The
Elves
and the
Shoemaker

The poor shoemaker gave a deep
sigh. Since the big shoe factory
opened up in town, people had stopped
coming to his little workshop.

With business so bad, the shoemaker couldn't afford to buy any more leather. Now there was just enough left to make one more pair of shoes.

Carefully, he cut out the shapes of the shoes and laid the pieces on the workbench. "I'll sew them together tomorrow," he said wearily. Then, with a heavy heart, he went up to bed.

When the shoemaker came downstairs in the morning, he rubbed his eyes in disbelief. Lying there on the workbench was a perfect pair of finished shoes. "I wonder how they got there," he muttered.

He picked up the shoes and stared at them. The stitches were the tiniest he'd ever seen, and every single one was as neat as could be. "How strange," he said, shaking his head. "I must still be dreaming."

"Dreaming about what?" asked his wife, popping her head around the door.

The shoemaker told her what had happened and she was just as puzzled as he was. But they put the shoes in the window in pride of place.

A few minutes later the bell rang and in walked an elegantly dressed gentleman. "I'd like to try on those magnificent shoes," he said.

"Certainly, sir," said the shoemaker. He and his wife bustled around. It was their first customer in a very long time and they were eager to please him.

The shoes were a perfect fit. It was as if they were made for him. "I'll take them," he declared, and he paid for them at once.

With the money, the shoemaker was able to buy leather for two more pairs of shoes.

That evening, he cut out the shapes of the new shoes. But, after all the excitement, he was exhausted. "Why don't you finish them in the morning?" suggested his wife.

"Good idea," said the shoemaker, and he and his wife went happily to bed.

The next morning, the shoemaker found two pairs of newly made shoes waiting for him. They had criss-cross ribbons and were decorated with sparkly sequins. "Goodness me," he exclaimed. "They're even better than the first pair."

No sooner had he put them in the window than they caught the attention of two sisters who were passing by. Now these sisters adored shoes. They had a hundred pairs each already, but none were as beautiful as these. In any case, they firmly believed that you could never have too many shoes.

They stood for a moment, drooling over them. "We have to have them," gushed the first sister. "They're simply divine!"

"No doubt about it," agreed the second. "We can't live without them."

Without further delay, they marched inside. "We'd like to try on those shoes in the window," they announced.

"Certainly, ladies," said the shoemaker. "Just give me a moment."

By the time he turned around with the shoes, the two sisters were already waiting in their stockinged feet, wiggling their toes in anticipation.

They slipped the shoes on and shrieked with excitement. Then they sprang to their feet and teetered around the workshop, giggling and doing little twirls.

The money the sisters paid was enough for the shoemaker to buy leather for four more pairs of shoes. He cut out the shapes, just as before, and then he and his wife went to bed.

By morning, there were four pairs of newly made shoes lined up on the workbench. They had towering heels and were embroidered all over with intricate patterns.

The shoemaker gazed at them admiringly. Then he wandered over to the window and opened the blinds. He almost jumped out of his battered old boots with shock.

A crowd of people had gathered, their noses pressed right up against the glass. As soon as he opened the door, they barged past, bashing with their handbags, poking with their umbrellas, and elbowing with their elbows.

Four lucky customers snatched up the shoes. "We want shoes! We want shoes!" chanted the others impatiently.

"Hold on!" cried the shoemaker's wife. "There'll be more shoes tomorrow."

The next day, customers were lined up all the way around the corner.

And so it went on. Every night the shoemaker cut out the leather and every morning the new shoes were waiting.

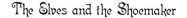

There were shoes
with buckles and shoes
with bows, knee-high boots with
pointy toes, clippety clogs and dainty
slippers, dancing pumps and winkle-pickers.

For a long time, the shoemaker and his wife
didn't dare to speak about what had happened
in case their good fortune came to an end.

Then, one evening, as they were closing up
the workshop, the shoemaker's wife asked,
"Who do you think is helping us?"

"I've been wondering the same thing," said the shoemaker. "Let's stay up tonight and see."

So, that night, instead of climbing the stairs to bed, they hid themselves in the next room and waited to see what would happen.

Just as the clock struck midnight, the door swung open and two little people, no higher than the shoemaker's knee, ran in. They were dressed in raggedy clothes and their feet were bare.

"Of course...elves!" whispered the shoemaker excitedly. "I should have guessed from those tiny stitches."

The elves climbed onto the workbench and set to work at once.

The shoemaker and his wife watched in amazement as their needles flew in and out, flashing like little lightning bolts.

The Elves and the Shoemaker

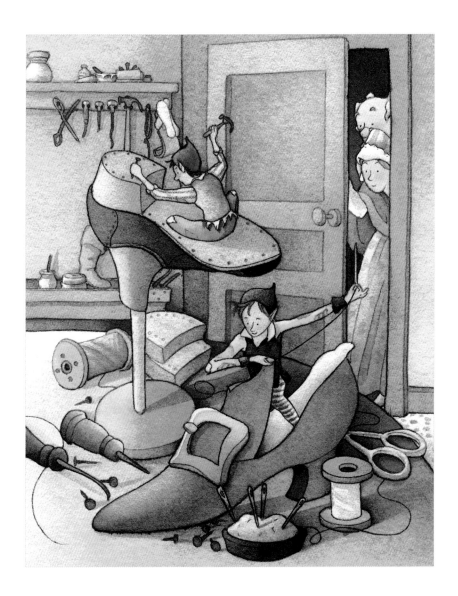

In no time at all, the two elves had made
a beautiful pair of shoes. They hammered on
the soles with a rat-a-tat-tat and polished
the shoes until they shone.

They quickly moved on to the next pair, and
the next and the next. The busy little elves didn't
stop until they had used up every single
piece of leather.

Only then did they stand back to admire
their work. "You know, I think these are even
better than Cinderella's shoes," said one.

"I quite agree," replied the other. "Glass
slippers are very pretty and all that, but these
are much more comfortable."

Looking rather pleased with themselves,
the elves jumped down from the workbench
and slipped out through the open door.

"Poor little things," said the shoemaker's wife when they'd gone. "Did you see their tattered clothes? We should make them some new ones to say thank you."

"What a splendid idea," said her husband. "I can't wait to see their faces."

Early the next morning, the two of them set to work. The shoemaker's wife sewed two neat little shirts, two handsome pairs of trousers, two stylish waistcoats, and two tiny pointed hats.

Meanwhile, the shoemaker cut out the pieces for two pairs of elfin boots and began to stitch them together. It was fiddly work, but he put his heart and soul into it.

The boots were made of shiny red leather, with turned-up toes and dainty golden bells all around the top.

By the time the shoemaker had finished, his eyes ached and his fingers bled. "I do hope they like them," he said anxiously.

That night, the shoemaker and his wife laid the clothes and boots out on the workbench. Then they hid in the corner of the workshop to wait for the elves.

When midnight chimed, the elves raced in, ready to start work. But, instead of pieces of leather, they found two little piles of clothes.

With squeals of delight, they pounced on their new outfits and put them on.

"Look at that handsome young fellow!" exclaimed one of the elves, admiring himself in the mirror.

The other elf chuckled. "We're much too elegant to work now," he said. "I think our cobbling days are over." Then he noticed the boots. "Ooooh, look," he gasped. "Do you think they're for us?"

"Well, I can't see them fitting anybody else around here, can you?" teased his friend.

The shoemaker held his breath as the elves examined the boots. They turned them over and looked at them every which way.

"Magnificent," declared the first elf at last. "What fine workmanship."

"Quite extraordinary," agreed the second. "I had no idea that humans were so talented."

They slipped their feet into the boots and clicked the heels together. Then they started to dance. They did a little jig along the workbench, turned cartwheels across the floor and skipped right out of the workshop door, with their golden bells jingling merrily.

The shoemaker looked at his wife and smiled. "I think they're happy customers," he said.

That was the last they saw of their little helpers. But it wasn't the end of the fairytale. The shoemaker continued making beautiful shoes and he always had plenty of customers. He and his wife were never poor again.

Snow White
and the
Seven Dwarfs

One winter's morning, the queen was sitting beside her window sewing when it began to snow. The snowflakes drifted like feathers down from the sky and settled on the window ledge.

As the queen watched them, her needle
slipped and pricked her finger. Three drops of
blood fell onto the snow.

"I wish I had a child," she sighed, "with skin
as white as snow, lips as red as blood, and hair as
black as the ebony wood of the window frame."

Nine months later
the queen's wish came
true and she gave birth
to a baby girl.

The king was
delighted. "Let's call
her Snow White,"
he suggested.

But the king's happiness didn't last long.
The queen became very ill and within a week she
had died. He and Snow White were all alone.

The king was desperately sad. He loved Snow White dearly, but he couldn't take care of her by himself. "A little girl needs a mother," he said.

So, after a year had passed, he decided to marry again. His new wife was beautiful, but she was also proud and vain. She couldn't bear the idea of anybody being more beautiful than her.

She even had a magic mirror, just to be absolutely sure. Every day, she would gaze into it and say, "Mirror, mirror, on the wall, who is the fairest of us all?"

And the mirror always answered, "You are, my queen." Then the queen was satisfied, for she knew the mirror always told the truth.

The queen had nothing to do with Snow White while she was growing up. She detested children and wanted the king all to herself.

So she didn't notice that as the years went
by Snow White became prettier and prettier.
Her ebony hair tumbled down over her
shoulders, framing her delicate face, and her
red lips grew soft and full.

Then, one dark day, the queen
stared into her mirror and asked,
"Mirror, mirror, on the wall,
who is the fairest of us all?"

She folded her arms smugly,
expecting the usual answer.
But, instead, the mirror
replied, "You are fair of
course, my queen, but Snow
White is the fairest of all."

"Snow White!"
screeched the queen.

Her face turned white with shock, then purple with rage, and finally green with envy. "There must be some mistake," she snarled.

"I don't make mistakes," said the mirror calmly. "See for yourself."

The queen looked out of the window and saw Snow White chasing butterflies by the fountain. Her eyes narrowed. It was true. Snow White was more beautiful.

Over the next few weeks, the queen asked the mirror again and again, but the answer was always the same. Jealousy coiled around her heart like a snake. "I must get rid of her," she decided.

Without telling the king of her plans, she called for the court huntsman. "Take Snow White into the forest and kill her," she ordered. "I can't bear to look at her any longer."

The huntsman was horrified. "But Your Majesty..." he began.

"Don't you dare disobey me," thundered the queen. "In fact, bring me back her lungs and liver, so that I can be sure she's dead."

So, early the next morning, the huntsman took Snow White with him. They rode over the hills until they reached a forest. Snow White chattered away happily, asking him about the animals and the trees. But the huntsman hardly said a word.

Eventually, they came to a part of the forest where the trees grew closer together. "Let's stop here," said the huntsman. They got down and he looked around nervously before pulling his hunting knife out of his belt.

"Is something wrong?" asked Snow White.

"The queen has ordered me to kill you," he said quietly.

Snow White shrank back in fear. "But why?" she cried. "What have I done?"

"I'm sorry," said the huntsman, hanging his head in shame. "I'm just following orders."

Tears welled up in Snow White's eyes. "Please don't kill me," she begged. "I'll run away into the forest. She'll never know the truth."

The huntsman's heart filled with pity. He was afraid for his own life, but he couldn't bring himself to kill her.

Just then, he saw a wild boar in the bushes. It gave him an idea. "Run, child," he urged, "but you must never come back to the palace or the queen will kill us both."

Snow White took a few steps. Then she stopped and looked back at him. "Thank you," she said softly. "You're a very kind man."

The huntsman watched her disappear between the trees. "Poor girl," he thought. "What will become of her?"

Swinging back onto his horse, the huntsman rode after the boar. When he caught up with it, he thrust with his sword, piercing its bristly skin. The boar let out an ear-splitting squeal.

As quickly as he could, the huntsman finished the creature off. Then he cut out its lungs and liver and took them to the queen, so that she would think Snow White was dead.

Meanwhile, Snow White wandered further into the gloomy forest. By now, it was growing dark and she was very frightened. She heard a rustle among the bushes and broke into a run.

Snow White ran and ran, stumbling over tangled tree roots and jagged stones. Shadowy branches reached out as if they were trying to catch hold of her.

She hardly knew which way to run, but she kept on going. Then, at last, she saw a pretty little cottage through the trees. She ran towards it and banged on the door. "Is there anyone at home?" she panted.

There was no answer, so Snow White pushed the door open. Inside, there was a little table surrounded by seven little chairs. It was laid out for supper with a neat, white tablecloth, seven

little plates piled up with bread and cheese, and seven little mugs filled with frothy milk.

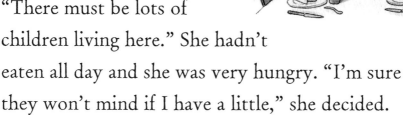

"How strange," thought Snow White. "There must be lots of children living here." She hadn't eaten all day and she was very hungry. "I'm sure they won't mind if I have a little," she decided.

But, not wanting to be rude, she helped herself to just a little bread and cheese from each plate and took only a sip of milk from each mug.

In the next room, Snow White found seven tidy little beds lined up in a row. After all the running she'd done, she was exhausted. "I think I'll lie down for a moment," she said.

She tried the first bed, but it was too short. The second was too low, the third too narrow, the fourth too soft, the fifth too hard and the sixth too lumpy. Luckily, the seventh one was just right. She curled up under the covers and fell fast asleep.

A little while later, the door of the cottage opened and in marched seven dwarfs. They realized at once that someone had been there.

"Who's been sitting on my chair?" demanded the first dwarf.

"Who's been eating off my plate?" asked the second.

"…and stealing my bread?" added the third.

"…and nibbling my cheese?" said the fourth.

"…and using my fork?" grumbled the fifth.

"…and my knife?" protested the sixth.

"…and drinking my milk?" complained the seventh.

Then the first dwarf went into the bedroom and found a hollow dip in his sheets. He touched it and found that it was still warm. "Who's been lying on my bed?" he cried out.

"Mine too, mine too!" they each exclaimed in turn. But the seventh dwarf just stared. "Who's this in my bed?" he said slowly.

The other six dwarfs hurried over. There lay Snow White, with her skin as white as snow, lips as red as blood, and hair as black as ebony. "Oooh," they all sighed. "She's lovely."

Snow White woke up the next morning to the clattering of dishes and the sound of merry whistling. She popped her head around the door and saw not seven children, but seven dwarfs.

At first, she was a little nervous, but they were so friendly and welcoming that she soon felt right at home. They all had breakfast together and she told them her story.

"Your stepmother sounds like a nasty piece of work," they said when she had finished. "But never mind. You'll be safe here with us."

After breakfast, the dwarfs slung their pickaxes over their shoulders and set off into the hills to dig for gold.

"Don't answer the door," they warned. "Your stepmother might come looking for you."

"I won't," promised Snow White.

Meanwhile, back at the palace, the queen didn't suspect a thing. The huntsman had given her the boar's lungs and liver, and she believed that Snow White was dead.

She went to her mirror and asked, "Mirror, mirror, on the wall, who is the fairest of us all?"

"You are the fairest here, my queen," began the mirror, "but Snow White is the fairest of all."

The queen stared in disbelief. "But Snow White is dead," she snarled.

"No, no," replied the mirror. "Snow White is alive and well. She's living in the forest with the seven dwarfs."

When the queen realized the huntsman
had lied, she was furious. Muttering to herself,
she paced up and down in front of the mirror.

Soon, she came up with a plan. She disguised
herself as a peasant
woman, filled a basket
with silk ribbons and set
off for the dwarfs' house.

Snow White was busy
cleaning the cottage when
she heard a knock at
the door. "Pretty things to
sell," croaked the queen.

Remembering the dwarfs' warning, Snow
White peered out of the window. But, when
she saw that it was just a harmless old woman,
she unbolted the door.

"My dear, I have just the thing for you," said the queen, pulling out a long, red ribbon. "Here, try it on." Quickly, she looped the ribbon around Snow White's waist and laced it up.

She pulled tighter and tighter until Snow White could no longer breathe. The girl turned pale and collapsed on the ground.

"That's dealt with the little fool," sneered the queen, and hurried back to the palace.

When the dwarfs returned a little while later, they were shocked to find Snow White lying on the ground. For a moment, they thought she was dead. Then they saw how tightly the ribbon was tied.

One of them whipped out a pocket knife and cut through it. Snow White spluttered and sat up. "You've saved my life," she gasped.

When Snow White had recovered, she told them about the old woman selling ribbons.

The dwarfs shook their heads. "That must have been the wicked queen," they said. "If she finds out you're not dead, she's bound to come back and try again."

I know," whispered Snow White fearfully. "I'll be more careful in the future."

By now, the queen was already back at the palace. She rushed straight to her mirror. "Mirror, mirror, on the wall, who is the fairest of us all?" she demanded.

Once again, the mirror answered, "You are the fairest here, my queen, but Snow White is the fairest of all."

"What does it take to put a stop to that girl?" hissed the queen.

The next day, she returned to the cottage with a new disguise and a poisonous comb.

"I'm afraid I can't let you in," said Snow White when she knocked at the door.

"I understand," said her stepmother. "You can't be too careful these days." She held up the comb and gave a sinister smile. "Still, there's nothing to stop you from looking at my wares."

"No, I suppose not," said Snow White, opening the door just a little.

The queen pushed forward. "Here, let me untangle your hair," she said. But the moment the comb touched Snow White's head, the girl slumped to the ground.

As soon as the dwarfs saw Snow White, they realized with horror that her stepmother had visited again.

They found the poisonous comb and pulled it out. Snow White's eyes flickered open. "My head hurts," she murmured.

"Your stepmother has been up to her tricks again," said the dwarfs. "You really must be more careful. While we're out, don't open the door to anyone."

"I won't," promised Snow White.

When the queen got home, she hurried to her mirror. "Mirror, mirror, on the wall, who is the fairest of us all?" she asked eagerly.

Yet again, the mirror answered, "You are the fairest here, my queen, but Snow White is the fairest of all."

"What???" shrieked the queen, trembling with rage. "That wretched girl. I'll finish her off if it's the last thing I do."

She mixed together all kinds of
potions to make a deadly poison.
Then she took an apple and
dipped the rosy-red side into
the mixture.

"You won't get away
so easily this time, my
pretty Snow White,"
she muttered.

Then, she put on
a new disguise and hurried to the dwarfs'
cottage. When she knocked at the door, Snow
White didn't answer it. "I'm sorry, I can't buy
anything today," she called.

"I'm not selling anything," said the queen
quickly. "I've picked so many apples I can't eat
them all. I thought you might like a few."

"Oh, I see," said Snow White, opening the window. "Well, it's very kind of you, but I'm afraid I really can't accept them."

"Are you afraid I'll poison you?" chuckled the queen. "Look, why don't we share one?" She cut the poisoned apple in two and ate one half herself. Then she held out the rosy-red half.

It looked so deliciously juicy that Snow White couldn't resist. She reached out and took it. But no sooner had she bitten into the apple than she collapsed on the ground. "Let's see who's the fairest now," crowed the queen.

Soon, the dwarfs came home and found Snow White. "Not again," they groaned. They checked for too-tight ribbons and poisonous combs, but they couldn't find what was wrong. "The wicked queen has killed her," they sobbed.

Meanwhile, the queen was standing triumphantly in front of her mirror. This time she was sure she had killed Snow White. "Mirror, mirror, on the wall, who is the fairest of us all?" she asked.

Sure enough, the mirror answered, "Now that Snow White is off the scene, you are the fairest of all, my queen."

"Just as it should be," said the queen with a hollow laugh.

Back in the forest, the dwarfs were still weeping. They couldn't bear the idea of burying Snow White under the ground. So, instead, they made a glass coffin and put it in the garden among the flowers she loved so much.

Each day, one of them would keep watch over her coffin while the others went off to work.

Months passed and Snow White didn't change a bit. Even in death, her skin was as white as snow, her lips were as red as blood, and her hair was as black as ebony.

Then, one day, a young prince rode by. When he saw the coffin, he stopped and got down from his horse. "Who is she?" he whispered, kneeling down beside her.

"It's our beloved Snow White," answered the dwarf who was guarding the coffin.

"Beauty like this belongs in a palace," said the prince. "Let me take her with me."

The dwarf shook his head. "We wouldn't part with her for all the world," he said.

"Then I will stay here too," said the prince.

When the other dwarfs returned, they felt sorry for the prince. "It's true," they admitted sadly. "She doesn't belong here." So, eventually, they agreed to let him take her to his palace.

The prince sent for his servants to carry the coffin. Carefully, they picked it up and put it on their shoulders. But, as they set off, one of them stumbled on a tree root.

The jolt dislodged the piece of poisoned apple from Snow White's mouth and out it flew. To the dwarfs' astonishment, her eyes opened. "She's alive!" they cried.

The prince opened the lid of the coffin and gazed down at Snow White. "Where am I?" she said in confusion.

"Don't worry," said the prince gently. "You're safe now."

Snow White and the Seven Dwarfs

Snow White looked into the prince's kind eyes and smiled. "I don't think we've met," she said.

"He's a prince," interrupted the dwarf who'd been guarding her. "I think he's in love with you."

The prince blushed. "I must admit it's true," he said. "I can't bear to leave you. Will you come home with me to my palace?"

Snow White glanced at the dwarfs and they nodded their encouragement. "I'd like that," she answered shyly.

She hugged each of the dwarfs in turn and said a tearful goodbye. Then the prince swept her up onto his horse and they rode away together.

A few weeks later, the prince and Snow White announced they were getting married. The happy news spread quickly and there were celebrations all across the land.

But one person wasn't at all happy. The queen stormed to her mirror and demanded, "Mirror, mirror, on the wall, who is the fairest of us all?"

There was a pause. The glass misted over and there before her appeared Snow White and her prince, with rose petals showering down upon them. "Snow White is the fairest," answered the mirror firmly, "of that there's no doubt."

The mist faded and the queen saw her own face staring back, hideously twisted with jealousy. "Nooooooo!" she shrieked, hurling the mirror across the room. As it smashed, a piece of glass flew out and pierced her wicked heart. "I knew that girl would be the end of me," she wailed, and she sank to the floor, stone cold dead.

The Brothers Grimm

Once upon a time, around two hundred years ago, there were two brothers who loved listening to stories. Their names were Jacob and Wilhelm Grimm.

In 1806, the brothers Grimm began collecting traditional German fairy tales.

They lived in Kassel, in the German state of Hesse, where they worked as librarians. At that time, Germany was made up of 39 separate states.

In 1806, the armies of the French dictator Napoleon overran the German states and took control. For the next six years, Napoleon's government suppressed local culture, which the Grimm brothers were working hard to keep alive.

As well as searching for forgotten stories in letters, books and medieval manuscripts in libraries, Jacob and Wilhelm invited storytellers to their home. According to Jacob, they wrote down everything they heard, "faithfully and truly, without embellishment and additions."

Some of the storytellers sound like characters from the fairy tales themselves. Many of the first tales the Grimms recorded came from Katherina

Viehmann, a widow from Kassel. Her father had been an innkeeper, so she had grown up listening to the tales told by wayfarers stopping off along the road to Frankfurt.

Other tales came from a poor, retired soldier, who gave the brothers stories in exchange for some of their old clothes. Friends of the family, and their servants, provided lots of stories too.

The brothers Grimm published their first collection of fairy tales at Christmas time, in 1812. It contained 86 stories, and was an instant success, and they brought out a second volume three years later.

As boys, Jacob and Wilhelm had slept in the same bed and done their school work at the same table; as students they had shared a room. They were seldom parted as adults either. So when Wilhelm married Dorothea Wild, a childhood friend who had provided the brothers with a dozen or so stories herself, it was only natural that Jacob should move in with them.

The brothers continued to live and work together for the rest of their lives. As well as the fairy tales, they published a vast collection of German legends and several books on languages and grammar. In later life, they also began researching and writing a huge dictionary of the German language, tracing the origin of every word – though this enormous project wasn't completed in their lifetimes.

But it was the fairy tales that made the Grimms famous around the world. They kept making changes and adding more stories to the collection. By the time they published their final edition of the fairy tales in 1857, it contained more than 200 stories.

In 1859, Wilhelm died. His brother paid tribute to him as, "a fairy tale brother". Jacob continued working on the dictionary, but died four years after his brother.

Since then, the fairy tales collected by the Grimms have been read and retold countless times all over the world, and translated into many different languages.

The stories in this book are just some of the tales that might have been forgotten forever, if it hadn't been for the brothers Grimm.

Timeline of the lives of the Brothers Grimm

1785 Jacob is born on the 4th of January, in Hanau, a town in the German state of Hesse.

1786 Wilhelm is born on the 24th of February.

1796 The Grimms' father dies. The family is left in financial difficulty, but an aunt pays for Jacob and Wilhelm to go to school in Kassel.

1802 Jacob moves to Marburg to study law. Wilhelm joins him a year later.

1806 Jacob and Wilhelm begin collecting stories.

1806-1813 The German states are invaded and occupied by the French armies of Napoleon.

1808 The Grimms' mother dies. Jacob gives up his studies and takes a job as a librarian in Kassel to support his younger brothers and sister.

1812 The Brothers Grimm publish *Children's and Household Tales*. It contains 86 of their collected stories.

1815 The Grimms publish the second edition of their fairytale collection, with 70 additional stories.

1819 Jacob publishes a study of German grammar.

1825 The Grimms publish a small edition of 50 tales, illustrated by their brother, Ludwig. Wilhelm marries Dorothea Wild.

1829 The brothers take up posts as librarian-professors at the University of Göttingen.

1837 The Grimms refuse to swear allegiance to the king of Hanover and lose their jobs.

1841 The Grimms take up positions as professors at the University of Berlin.

1848 Jacob publishes a history of the German language, then retires.

1852 Wilhelm retires. The brothers begin working together on a complete German dictionary.

1857 The Grimms publish the final edition of their fairy tale collection. It contains 200 stories, and 10 children's legends.

1859 Wilhelm dies on the 16th of December, aged 73.

1863 Jacob dies on the 20th of September, aged 78.

Edited by Anna Milbourne
Designed by Mary Cartwright and Jessica Johnson
Digital design by John Russell

This edition first published in 2010 by Usborne Publishing Ltd, 83-85 Saffron Hill, London EC1N 8RT, England. www.usborne.com Copyright © 2010 Usborne Publishing Ltd. The name Usborne and the devices ♀🌐 are Trade Marks of Usborne Publishing Ltd. First published in America in 2011. U.E.